The Night the
New Jesus
Fell to Earth

SOUTHERN REVIVAL SERIES

Robert H. Brinkmeyer, Jr., Series Editor

The Night the New Jesus Fell to

Earth
And Other Stories from Cliffside, North Carolina

Ron Rash   New Introduction by the Author

THE UNIVERSITY OF SOUTH CAROLINA PRESS

*Published in Cooperation with the Institute for
Southern Studies of the University of South Carolina*

Original edition published by The Bench Press
New edition published by the University of South Carolina Press
Columbia, South Carolina 29208

www.sc.edu/uscpress

Manufactured in the United States of America

24 23 22 21 20 19 18 17 16 15
10 9 8 7 6 5 4 3 2 1

Library of Congress Cataloging-in-Publication Data
can be found at http://catalog.loc.gov/.

ISBN: 978-1-61117-514-1 (pbk)

This book was printed on recycled paper with 30 percent
postconsumer waste content.

For my teachers

Contents

Acknowledgments

The author would like to thank the following for valuable advice and assistance: Fran Crocker, Bill Koon, Ann Rash, and Mark Steadman.

Grateful acknowledgement is made to the following for permission to reprint previously published material:
  Charleston Magazine, "Love and Pain in the
    New South"
  A *Carolina Literary Companion*, "The Night the New
    Jesus Fell to Earth in Cliffside, North Carolina" and
    "Raising the Dead in Cliffside, North Carolina"
  A *Fireside Companion*, "My Father's Cadillacs"
  The *State* newspaper, "Yard of the Month"

"The Night the New Jesus Fell to Earth in Cliffside, North Carolina" won a General Electric Younger Writers Award. "Yard of the Month" won a South Carolina Arts Commission Prize.

Sponsored by the Richland-Lexington Cultural Council, the original publication of this book was funded in part by the South Carolina Arts Commission, which receives support from the National Endowment for the Arts.

Series Editor's Preface

Southern Revivals, supported by the University of South Carolina Institute for Southern Studies's Robert E. McNair Fund, restores to print important works of literature by contemporary southern writers. All selections in the series have enjoyed critical and commercial success. By returning these works to general circulation, we hope to deepen readers' understandings of, and appreciations for, not only specific authors but also the flourishing southern literary landscape. Not too long ago, it was a fairly straightforward task to distinguish literature by southerners, as most of their works focused on easily recognizable "southern" themes, perspectives, and settings. Those days are long gone. Literature by southerners is now quite literally all over the map, extending its reach from the coast of South Carolina to heart of West Africa, from the bayous of Louisiana to the rain forests of Brazil, from the mountains of Eastern Tennessee to the deserts of the Southwest. As our list of resurrected books grows, Southern Revivals will bring readers to many of these places, taking them on journeys into regions near and far away, journeys which attest to the astonishing diversity of contemporary Southern culture.

Ron Rash's *The Night the New Jesus Fell to Earth and Other Stories from Cliffside, North Carolina* is an exciting addition to the series. Few would disagree that Rash is one of the South's—and the nation's—most important contemporary writers. Since the publication in 1994 of *The Night the New Jesus Fell to Earth*, which was Rash's first book, he has gone on to publish four other collections of stories, four collections of poetry, a children's book, and five novels, perhaps most notably *Serena*, to my eyes one of the most powerful and rich novels by an American writer to appear in the last decade. Prestigious awards have been piling up almost from the very beginning of Rash's career; these include, among many others, the Sherwood Anderson Prize, the James Still Award from the Fellowship of Southern Writers, and the Frank O'Connor International Short Story Award. Originally from Chester, South Carolina, in 2010 Rash was inducted into South Carolina Academy of Authors.

The Night the New Jesus Fell to Earth is a set of linked stories, told alternately by three narrators during a long night of talk following the destruction by fire of Greene's Café, one of the mainstay establishments of the small town of Cliffside. The tales told by the three narrators— Vincent, Tracy, and Randy—all zero in on crucial moments in their lives and progress chronologically, moving toward the present day. Although the stories are often serious in subject, everything from the struggle to survive a deadly snakebite, to the tribulations of a nasty divorce, to the suffering—both professional and personal—from malicious rumors and innuendos, the narrators spin their tales with a downhome appreciation of the quirky, if not zany, ways of small-town life. In other words the stories are finally profoundly comic, celebrating the narrators' efforts to work through the inevitable changes that rock their lives. That comic vision can be seen in the language itself, as when Randy describes the downfall of his marriage after he accidentally puts his wife's pet monkey in a washing machine: "The marriage was as good as over by the rinse cycle." Or when Tracy describes the frequency of a church-hopping couple by saying, "They changed churches more often than most people change their oil filters."

The backdrop to the narrators' wrenching personal crises is the subtle, yet over time equally momentous, transformation that the town itself is undergoing. Here is how Randy puts it, as he sips on some moonshine: "So much is changing down here so fast people will buy anything that makes them feel like they're living in the South instead of some southern suburb of New Jersey. Southerners aren't worth a damn when it comes to change, and that's why God gave us moonshine and people like Junior to make it." Even Vincent, who, growing up in the tumultuous 1960s, finds a measure of security in how slowly the town is changing, knows that a wind is blowing that will eventually sweep aside the old ways. Most of the adults in town, Vincent observes, are merely biding their time, "content to let the town drag its heels, to hold out as long as possible."

As dawn breaks after their night of storytelling, Vincent, Tracy, and Randy depart, going their own separate ways, heading out to their everyday chores and responsibilities. They have clearly enjoyed their night of fellowship; but it is also clear that such fellowship has now become rare, with the atomization not only of their lives but also of Cliffside itself, a point underscored in the event that brought them together: the destruction of the town's regular gathering spot. As Tracy drives off to work, she passes by the burnt-out shell of Greene's, seeing the regulars milling about, looking "like they still can't believe it's gone, like the fire was just a bad dream." Tracy eventually turns out onto the highway, and, in *The Night the New Jesus Fell to Earth*'s final words, watches "Cliffside disappear in the rearview mirror."

Robert H. Brinkmeyer, Jr.

Introduction

The Night the New Jesus Fell to Earth began as an attempt to write a novel. I was twenty-two years old and working on an M.A. in English at Clemson University. The novel was centered on a young boy and a snow-cone salesman named Badeye. I wrote 150 pages or so, most of which were so bad that I threw the whole manuscript in a dumpster. A while later, however, I culled from memory enough of what I'd thrown away to write "Badeye," this collection's opening story. Not long after that I wrote "My Father's Cadillacs," and then the title story.

I have always loved *Winesburg, Ohio*, especially how those interwoven tales give the satisfaction of individual stories yet, ultimately, also a novelistic sense of a particular place. I wrote more "Cliffside" stories and had the collection largely finished by the time I was thirty; then, for the next decade, my focus turned to poetry. The Cliffside stories lay in a dresser drawer until Warren Slesinger at Bench Press expressed an interest in my fiction and I sent him the manuscript. I added another story and an italicized beginning and end that allowed the reader to imagine all the stories were told on one night, a southern *Decamaron*. I was forty-one when *The Night the New Jesus Fell to Earth* was finally published.

Over the years some of my early readers have noted that *The Night the New Jesus Fell to Earth* is much different from the fiction I have written since. "What happened to you; you were funny in your first book?" is the essence of the question I have been asked numerous times. "I had children," is my response, an answer that is meant to be humorous and is taken that way. But having revisited these stories, I suspect there is some truth to that comment. My son and daughter were wonderful children and have become wonderful adults. They are a source of great joy in my life, but I also know that, once they had been born, I became increasingly troubled about the world they were growing up in. In novels such as *Serena* and *The Cove*, I used the past as a prism to comment on contemporary issues, and, in story collections such as *Burning Bright* and *Nothing Gold Can Stay*, I addressed present issues more openly.

Yet now, as I reach the sixth decade of my life, I know that humor and wonder are a vital part of what art can give us, perhaps even more vital in troubled times. The great Arkansas writer Donald Harington once said that literature allows us "to better enjoy life or to better endure it." The novel I am now working on is primarily about wonder and how it can sustain us in the bleakest of circumstances. In some ways this new book is more akin to *The Night the New Jesus Fell to Earth* than any of my recent work. And so I return to where I started.

Revisiting one's novice work can be exasperating. Various shortcomings are anticipated and quickly confirmed. I turn one page and find a clunky sentence, on another a simile barnacled with cliché, a couple of instances where I wish I'd had a more mature, more enlightened sensibility. What I most feared finding, however, was the smug condescention young writers are too often prone to, particularly when writing about a place largely based on where they grew up. I am pleased to find little of that tone in this collection. What I find instead is that, despite their foibles, the residents are depicted not just sympathetically but fondly. I am glad that this is so, because I have immense gratitude for all that Boiling Springs, North Carolina, gave me. I doubt I would have become a writer had I not lived there.

Readers who come to this book for the time will find the flaws of a writer still learning his craft, but I also hope that they will find humor and, perhaps, a bit of wonder as well.

Ron Rash
March 2014

Prologue

I hear the fire alarm go off and I'm up, yanking off my nightgown and putting on a sweatshirt and some jeans. The clock glows three o'clock, but in a small town you get your excitement whatever hour you can. Besides, I'm a member of the volunteer fire department and might be needed. I hear the fire truck screaming towards town, so I head that way in my pickup. I park beside Benson's Drug Store. People are already starting to gather, a lot of curlers and bare feet. Out in the street in front of Greene's Cafe, Donnie Splawn and Phil Moore are arguing about how to unroll the fire hose, but they needn't bother. Greene's Café is nothing but smoke and ashes. Next to where the front door used to be, Carl Blowmeyer and my ex-husband are elbowing each other trying to get better shots with their camcorders, both figuring, I'm sure, that they can sell the footage to WSOC in Charlotte. Marvin Greene is sitting on the curb. He's got a pint of moonshine in his left hand that everybody including Sheriff Hawkins is pretending not to see. Marvin takes a swallow and raises the mason jar up towards what is left of his café. Then he tries to get up, which he does for about a half a second before he starts to wobble like a bowling pin that can't make up its mind to stand or fall. Vincent Hampton, who's home visiting his mother, and Randy

Ledbetter run over and steady Marvin. I walk over to help them out. The first thing I do is take the mason jar out of Marvin's hand and pour what's left in it out in the street. "What'd you do that for, Tracy?" Marvin says. "I've been saving that shine for thirty years for my retirement and now it's here. Too old to rebuild. Besides, that Shoney's is coming in the spring." I'm thinking if Marvin were ten years younger, I could help him rebuild. But he's right. He is too old to start again from scratch. By this time Marvin has closed his eyes. He'll have a few hours before he has to figure out what to do with the rest of his life. Sometimes that's enough, provided you can deal with the hangover. I tell Randy and Vincent we need to get Marvin home and into his bed. Vincent offers to drive his Coup De Ville, but he'll have to walk half a mile over to his mom's house to get it. I say let's take my truck instead, that I've got some quilts I can put in the truck bed. It may be a little bumpy, but Marvin's too pickled to notice. So Vincent and Randy lift him up and put him in the truck bed as gently as gently as they can. Randy says he'll follow me in his truck. Vincent says he'll ride with me, so he climbs in the cab and we head out Broad River Road toward Marvin's place. When we get there, I fish the key out of Marvin's pocket and open the door. Vincent and me carry him inside. Marvin mutters something about an order of fried chicken to go and needing to hide the mattress. The he starts snoring again. We lay him on the bed, take off his shoes, and put a blanket over him. Randy comes in and asks if me and Vincent want to come by his place for a cup of coffee before we head back to town, and I say sure it's too late to go back to sleep and Vincent says that's fine by him so we head on over the river to the old Caldwell farm, Randy's

2

place now. On the way there I ask Vincent how long he's going to be in town, and he says just the weekend. I ask him if he thinks he might ever move back to Cliffside, and he says he doubts it. He says Cliffside could never be the way it was when he grew up here. He says he and Cliffside have changed too much to be comfortable with one another, and he would rather remember Cliffside the way it used to be. Randy puts on a pot of coffee when we get there, and we all sit down at the kitchen table. There's no moon and it's dark as death outside, but Randy's kitchen is bright and cozy. We drink the coffee but that's just an excuse to do what folks always do around Cliffside when change happens. Somebody dying, somebody being born, whatever brings us out into the night. We start talking and soon the words turn into sentences and those sentences become stories. Always, finally, stories. . . .

I

Badeye

I remember Badeye Carter. I remember his clear blue eye, the patch, the serpent tattooed on his shoulder, the long, black fingernails. I remember his black '49 Ford pickup, the rusty cowbell dangling from the sideview mirror, the metal soft drink chest in the back filled with shaved ice, the three gallon jars of flavoring—cherry, lemon, and licorice, the Hav-a-Tampa cigar box he kept his money in. I remember how he always came that summer at bull-bat time, those last moments of daylight when the streetlight in our neighborhood came on and the bats began to swoop, preying on moths attracted to the glow.

That summer was the longest of my life. Time seemed to sleep that summer. Sometimes a single afternoon seemed a week. June was an eternity. It must have seemed just as endless to my mother, for this was the summer when my obsession with snakes reached its zenith, and our house seemed more a serpentarian than a home. And then there was Badeye, to my mother just as slippery, and as danger-ous.

I was eight years old. Every evening when I heard the clanging of the cowbell, I ran to the edge of the street, clutching the nickel I had begged from my father earlier that day. I never asked my mother. To her Badeye was an intruder, a bringer of tooth decay, bad eating habits, and other things.

Every other mother in Cliffside felt the same way, would refuse to acknowledge Badeye's hat-tipping "how you doing, ma'ams" as he stopped his truck in front of their houses. They would either stare right at him with a look colder than anything he ever put in his paper cones, as my mother did, or, like our next door neighbor Betty Splawn, turn her back to him and walk into the house.

Their reasons for disliking Badeye went beyond his selling snowcones to their children. They knew, as everyone in Cliffside knew, that while Badeye was new to the snowcone business, he had been the town's bootlegger for over a decade. Being hard-shell Southern Baptists, these women held him responsible for endangering their husband's eternal souls with his moonshine brought up from Scotland County.

There was also the matter of his right eye, which had been blinded ten years earlier when Badeye's wife stabbed him with an icepick as he slept. Badeye had not pressed charges, and the ex-Mrs. Carter had not explained her motivation before heading for Alabama to live with a sister, leaving the women of Cliffside to wonder what *he* must have done to deserve such an awakening.

Cliffside's fathers viewed Badeye more sympathetically. They tended to believe his snowcones would cause no lasting harm to their children, sometimes even eating one themselves. As for the bootlegging, some of these men were Badeye's customers, but even those who did not drink, such as my father, felt Badeye was a necessary evil in a town where the nearest legal alcohol was fifteen miles away. These men also realized that each of them had probably done something during their years of marriage that warranted an icepick in the eye. Badeye's right eye had died for all their sins.

So it was our fathers we went to, waiting until our mothers were washing the supper dishes or were otherwise occupied. Our fathers would fish out nickels from their pants pockets, trying not to jingle the change too loudly, listening, like us, for the sound of our mothers' approaching footsteps.

Badeye always stopped between our house and the Splawns'. Donnie Splawn, who was my age, his younger brother, Robbie, and I would gather around the tailgate of Badeye's truck, our bare feet burning on the still-hot pavement. Sometimes we would be joined by another child, one who had gotten his nickel only after Badeye had passed by his house, forced to chase the truck through the darkening streets, finally catching up with him in front of our houses. It was worth it—that long, breathless run we had all made at some time when our mothers had not washed the dishes right away or when we had been playing and did not hear the cowbell until too late, worth it because Badeye's snowcones were the most wonderful thing we had ever sunk our teeth into.

Donnie and I were partial to cherry, while Robbie liked lemon best. Donnie and Robbie tended to suck the syrup out of their snowcones, while I let the syrup in mine pool in the bottom of the paper cone, a last, condensed gulp so flavorful that it brought tears to my eyes.

Our mothers tried to fight back. They first used time-honored scare tactics, handed down from mother to daughter for generations. My mother's version of the "trip to the dentist with snowcone-rotted teeth" horror story was vividly rendered, but while it did cause me to brush my teeth more frequently for a while, it did not slow my snowcone consumption. The story's only lasting impact on me was a lifelong fear of dentists.

When my mother realized this conventional story had failed, she assumed the cause was overexposure, that stories, like antibiotics, tended to become less effective on children the more they were used, so she came up with a new story, one unlike any heard in the collective memory of Cliffside's children. The story concerned an eight-year-old boy in the adjoining county who had contracted a rare disease carried specifically by flies that lit on snowcones. The affliction reduced the boy's backbone to jelly in a matter of days. He now spent all of his time in a wheelchair, looking mournfully out his bedroom window at all the non-snowcone-eating children who played happily in the park across the street from his house. The setting of the story in Rutherford County was a stroke of genius on my mother's part, for it helped create a feeling of "if it could happen there, it could happen here" while at the same time being far enough away from Cliffside so as not to be easily discredited. The park across the street also was a nice touch. But even at eight I realized the story was too vivid, the details too fully realized (my mother even knew the victim's middle name) to be anything other than fiction. I continued to eat Badeye's snowcones.

My mother, along with other mothers, realized another strategy was needed, so in an informal meeting after Sunday School in late June, Hazel Wasson, Dr. Wasson's wife, was appointed to find out if the law could accomplish what the horror stories had failed to do. Mrs. Wasson spent the following Monday morning in the county courthouse in Shelby. To her amazement as well as everyone else's, Badeye had all the necessary licenses to sell his snowcones. Mrs. Wasson's next stop, this time accompanied by Clytemnestra Ely, was to call on the county sheriff, who appeased the women by promising to conduct an illegal-liquor search on Badeye's premises the following afternoon, and, according to my mother, about thirty minutes after calling to let Badeye know they were coming. The sheriff and two of his deputies conducted their raid and claimed to have found nothing.

"I don't know why we even bothered to try," I heard my mother tell Betty Splawn the following morning, "what with Cleveland County politicians being his most loyal customers."

In the first week of July my mother spearheaded a last, concerted effort against Badeye. She found a recipe for freezing Kool-Aid in ice-cube trays. The cubes were then broken up in a blender or placed inside a plastic bag and crushed with a hammer. According to the final sentence of the recipe, which my mother chanted again and again, trying to convince not only me but herself as well, the result was "an inexpensive taste treat every bit as good as the commercial snowcone all children love." As the Kool-Aid hardened in the freezer, my mother called other mothers. By late afternoon every child in Cliffside had been served a dixie cup filled with my mother's recipe, but while we condescendingly ate these feeble imitations, they only served to whet our appetite for the real thing. My mother threw away the recipe and dumped the remaining trays of Kool-Aid cubes into the kitchen sink.

After this fiasco, Badeye seemed invincible. There were occasional minor victories: a husband might be coaxed or bullied into not giving his children nickels for a few days, or a son or daughter might wake up in the middle of the night with a toothache, which the mother could blame on Badeye's snowcones. The child would promise to repent, to never eat another one. But he or she always did, just as the fathers, after a day or two of ignoring their children's pleas, began to slip nickels to their offspring.

At my house, my mother had simply given up her battle against Badeye. Being a deeply religious person, she accepted the biblical edict that the husband was the decision-maker in a household. She could explain to my father the reasons she did not want me to eat Badeye's snowcones, but whether he gave me the nickels was a decision he as head of the household would have to make, and she would have to abide by that decision, no matter how wrongheaded it was.

There was also the matter of the weather. Our house, like almost all in Cliffside, was unairconditioned. The energy that had fueled my mother's horror stories and her recipe search was being steadily sapped away by the fierce heat of the North Carolina summer.

But, most of all, my mother had another problem that made Badeye seem little more than a nuisance—my growing snake collection. The previous summer I had caught a green snake in our backyard and brought it into our kitchen. My mother had screamed, dropped the plate she had been drying, and run out the front door. She did not stop running until she reached the Splawns' house, where she called my father at the junior college where he taught. My father rushed home and ran inside, my mother watching from the Splawns' front yard. When my father and I had come out a few minutes later, the snake was, to my mother's horror, still very much alive, though safely contained in a mason jar.

That snake was the first of a dozen garter and green snakes I would catch in our back and side yards that summer. Despite my mother's pleas, my father refused to kill them. Instead, he punched holes in the jar lids and encouraged me to keep them a couple of days before turning them loose again. My father tried to assure my mother, lectured her on the value of snakes, how most were nonpoisonous, were friends of mankind who helped control mice and rats. He had even brought a book on reptiles home from the college library to support his views. But my mother had her own book to refer to—the Bible, and in its first chapters found enough evidence to convince her that snakes had been, since the Garden of Eden, mankind's worst enemy. Now, with the aid of her husband, her son was making "pets" out of them, further proof to her of man's fallen nature.

My mother had hoped that my fascination with reptiles was, like the hula hoop, a passing fad that would be forgotten once the snakes went underground for the winter. This might have happened except for my father.

Up until this point in my life, my father and I had been rather distant. Part of the problem was that, possessing an artistic temperament, he was distant towards everyone, his mind fixed on some personal vision of truth and beauty. But even the times he had tried to establish some kind of rapport with me had been unsuccessful, since these attempts consisted of Saturday morning trips to the basement of the college's fine arts building. Once there my father sat me on a stool and placed a football-sized lump of clay in front of me, assuming that a five- or six-year-old boy would find a morning spent making pottery as enjoyable as he did.

He was wrong, of course. I quickly became bored and wished I were home watching cartoons. I watched the clock hands crawl towards lunchtime, daydreaming of fathers such as Mr. Splawn, who had taught Donnie how to throw a curve ball and took him bass fishing at Washburn's pond.

It was snakes that brought us together. To my amazement my father shared my interest in reptiles and even spoke of having caught snakes when he was a child. And it was he who, during that long, snakeless winter of my seventh year, kindled my interest with books checked out of the college's library.

By March I rivaled Dr. Brown, the college's biology teacher, as Cliffside's leading herpetologist. With my father's assistance, I had read every book on reptiles in Cliffside Junior College Library. I also owned a book on snakes better than any found there, a massive tome big as our family Bible, a Christmas present from my father titled *Snakes of the World.*

It was this book, more than anything else, that turned my hobby into an obsession. Unlike most of the books from the college's library which had small, black-and-white photographs, *Snakes of the World* had 14 x 8 inch color plates. Opening the dull reddish-brown cover of that book was the visual equivalent of biting into one of Badeye's snowcones, for though my mother could never have comprehended it, I found these creatures indescribably beautiful. Not all of them, of course. Some, like the water moccasins or timber rattlesnakes, had thick, bloated bodies and flattened heads and were black or dull brown. There were others, however, that were stunning in their beauty: the bright-green tree boa, for instance, found in the Amazon; or the gaboon viper, an Asian snake, its dark-blue color prettier than the stained glass windows of our church.

The most beautiful one of all, however, the coral snake, was not found in Australia, or Asia, or Africa but in the American South. A picture of a coral snake appeared on page 137 of my book, and in the right-hand corner of that page was a paragraph that I quickly memorized:

Because of its alternating bands of black, red, and yellow, the North American Coral Snake (*micrirus fulvius*) is one of the most brilliantly colored snakes in the world. A secretive, nocturnal creature found in the Southern United States, it is rarely encountered by humans. The North American Coral Snake is a member of the cobra family, and thus, despite its small size (rarely exceeding three feet in length), is the most venomous reptile in the Northern Hemisphere.

I celebrated my eighth birthday in late March. As the fried chicken cooled and the candles started to droop on top of the cake, my mother and I assumed my father was in the basement of the fine arts building throwing pots, having forgotten that it was his only child's birthday. But we were wrong. Just as we started to go ahead and eat, my father came in the back door, grinning, a wire mesh cage in his right hand. He placed it on the dining room table between the green beans and my cake.

"Happy Birthday, son," he said.

It took me a few seconds to identify the creature coiled in the bottom of the cage as a hog-nosed snake, but it only took my mother about half a second to drop her fork, shove back her chair, and make a frantic exit into the kitchen. After taking a minute to compose herself, she appeared at the doorway separating the kitchen from the dining room.

"I will not have a live snake inside my house, James," she said. "Either me or that snake is leaving right now."

It was clear my mother was not bluffing, so my father carried the cage out to the carport, moving some stacks of old art magazines to clear a space in the corner farthest from the door. When I asked my father where the snake had come from, he told me he had driven to Charlotte that afternoon and had visited three pet shops before finally finding what he wanted.

As March turned into April, the temperatures began to rise. The dogwood tree in our sideyard blossomed, and snakes began to crawl out of their burrows. Because my father had absolutely no interest in keeping up his property, our back and side yards were a kudzu-filled jungle, a reptile haven. It was here that I spent most of my spring afternoons. My reading had made me a much more successful snake hunter than I had been the previous summer. Instead of wandering around hoping to get lucky and spot a sunning snake, my method became much more sophisticated. I covered the back and side yards with large pieces of tin and wood as well as anything else that might provide a snake shelter. Each piece was placed carefully so that a snake could crawl under it with little difficulty. My efforts paid almost immediate dividends, for I now not only caught green snakes and garter snakes but also other species, including several small king snakes and, in late May, a five-foot-long black snake.

My father had borrowed a dozen wire cages from Dr. Brown, so I was able to keep the snakes I caught for several weeks at a time, longer if they ate well in captivity. I cleared out more space on the carport as I filled cage after cage. When school let out the first week of June, my snake-hunting range extended beyond my own yard. I caught thick-bodied water snakes in Sandy Run Creek, sleek, red-tongued green snakes in the vacant lot next to my grandmother's mill house in Shelby, orange and white corn snakes in my Uncle Earl's barn, tiny ring-necked snakes in the dense woods behind Laura Bryant's house. My father borrowed more cages from the high school.

By this time the hot weather had brought out Badeye as well, and for a while my mother fought a spirited battle against both, using similar tactics. Having grown up in the rural South, she had a rich repository of snake stories to draw on, so every night before I went to sleep, my mother would pull a chair beside my bed and try to frighten me out of my hobby. She told of timber rattlesnakes dropping out of trees, strangling children by wrapping around their necks, of copperheads lying camouflaged in leafpiles, waiting for someone to step close enough so they could inject their always-fatal poison, of blue racers, almost as poisonous as copperheads, so swift they could chase down the fastest man, and hoop snakes, capable of rolling up in a hoop, their tails poison-filled stingers.

My mother's bedtime stories were graphic, and there is little doubt that they would have cured most children of not only snake collecting but sleep as well. But I found them only humorous, even less convincing than her snowcone horror stories because I knew her tales had absolutely no basis in fact. Timber rattlesnakes did not climb trees, and they were vipers, not constrictors. Copperhead bites were rarely fatal, more often than not requiring little medical attention. Blue racers were non-poisonous, incapable of speeds greater than five miles an hour, even in short bursts. Hoop snakes were non-poisonous also, and unable to roll into a hoop, though as page 72 of *Snakes of the World* made clear, "Reports to the contrary continue to persist in primitive, superstitious regions of the United States."

My mother bought baseball cards and a half-dozen Indianhead pennies, trying to get me interested in collecting something besides snakes. She purchased a chemistry set, believing the possibility of my blowing myself up a lesser danger than my snake collecting. Her efforts were futile. I traded the baseball cards to Jimbo Miller for a half-dozen rat snake eggs he found in a sawdust pile and bought bubblegum with the pennies. The chemistry set gathered dust in the basement.

By this time my mother was having nightmares about snakes several times a week. Dark circles began to appear under her eyes. For the first time in my life, I watched her refuse to defer to my father, the view of serpents in Genesis evidently balancing out the command that wives should obey their husbands, the danger to her son tipping the scales. Every evening at supper she would lecture my father on the catastrophe that was about to occur.

Sometimes she even succeeded in breaking through the trance-like state he spent most of his waking hours in. At these times my father related the information he had gleaned from the books he had read to me the past winter. He tried to convince my mother that her fears were groundless, that the only poisonous snake in the county was the copperhead whose bite was rarely serious enough to require medical treatment, that the truly dangerous snakes—water moccasins, rattlesnakes, and coral snakes—were at least two counties away. He assured my mother that she didn't even have to worry about the copperheads because I had promised him that if I did come across one I would not try to catch it, would keep my distance.

My mother's sense of impending doom was not assuaged. Her fear of snakes was more than cultural and religious; it was instinctual as well, too deeply imbedded in her psyche to be dealt with on a rational level. Facts and statistics were useless. She threatened to get rid of the snakes, gather up the cages and take them away herself, but I knew she wouldn't do it, couldn't do it. Her fear of snakes was so great she had not even set foot on the carport since the arrival of the hog-nosed snake in March.

By the dog days of August I had thirty-three cages in the carport, and every one had a snake in it. The feeding of the snakes and the cleaning of the cages left me little time for snake-collecting field trips, but by this time the snakes were coming to me.

Not by themselves, of course, slithering by the hundreds toward our house. That occurred only in my mother's dreams. In late July Frank Moore, who owned, published, and wrote the *Cleveland County Messenger*, had done an article about me and my hobby, making me a county-wide celebrity and bringing a steady stream of visitors to our carport. Most came empty-handed, just wanting to see my collection, but others brought milk pails and wash buckets, mason jars and once even a cookie tin. Inside were snakes, some alive, some dead. The live ones I put in cages; the dead ones that were not too badly mangled by hoe, buckshot, or tire I placed, depending on their size, in quart or gallon jars filled with alcohol. Though months earlier my mother had told my father and me that she would not allow a "live" snake in her house, she had said nothing about dead ones, so I kept these snakes in my room where, almost every night, they crawled out of their jars and into my mother's dreams.

Badeye came too. One night after completing his rounds, he drove back by the house and, seeing me alone on the carport, parked his truck across the street. The carport lightbulb was burned out, the only light coming from the streetlight across the road, so I took each snake out of its cage so that Badeye could see them better. Unlike the other people who visited the carport that summer, Badeye did not keep his distance from the snakes once I took them into my hands. He moved closer, his blue eye only inches away as he studied each one intently.

When I had put the last snake back in its cage, Badeye rolled up one of the sleeves of his soiled, white t-shirt.

"Look here," he said, pointing to a king cobra, hood flared, tattooed on his upper arm. I moved closer and saw, incredibly, the cobra uncoil slightly, its great head sway back and forth. Badeye grinned as I stepped back, stumbled over a stack of newspapers.

"I've got to go," he said. "I've got a long drive downstate to make tonight." I watched him slowly walk back to the truck, slide behind the steering wheel, then disappear into the darkness. As I walked back to the carport, I saw my mother watching from the living room window. Tears flowed down her cheeks.

I did not sleep much that night. Part of the reason was

the heat. The temperature had been over ninety-five every day for three weeks. Rain was only a memory. The night brought no cool breezes, only more hot, stagnant air. But it was more than the heat. It was the cobra on Badeye's arm and my mother's tears. I sweated through the night as if I had a fever, listening to the window fan beat futilely against the darkness.

The following evening Badeye gave Donnie and Robbie their snowcones first, even though I had beaten them to his truck. After they left, Badeye jumped out of the truckbed and opened the door on the passenger side.

"I've got something for you," he said. "Saw it on the road last night when I was driving back from Laurinburg."

Badeye held an uncapped quart whiskey bottle up to my face.

"It's the prettiest snake I ever saw," he said.

And so it was, for a coral snake that looked to be a foot long lay in the bottom of the bottle.

"Is it alive?" I asked, hoping for a second miracle.

Badeye shook the bottle. The snake pushed its black head against the glass, tried to climb upwards before collapsing on itself.

"Here," he said, placing the bottle in my hand, though still gripping it with his own. "It's yours if you will do one thing for me."

"Anything," I said, meaning it.

"You know Bub Ely, don't you, and where he lives, that white house next to Marshall Hamrick's?"

I nodded. It was only a half mile away.

"Well, I need to get something to him, but I can't take it by right now." Badeye grinned. "His wife don't approve of me. Tonight, say about eleven, after everyone goes to sleep, could you take it over to his house? Just put it in the garage. Bub will find it in the morning."

I said I would. Badeye ungripped the whiskey bottle, opened the glove compartment.

"Here," he said, handing me a mason jar filled with a clear liquid that looked like water but I already knew had to be moonshine.

"You know what it is?" Badeye asked.

I nodded.

"Good," he said, sliding behind the steering wheel. "You'll know to be careful with it." Badeye's voice suddenly sounded menacing. "Don't get careless and drop it."

After checking to make sure my parents were not watching out the window, I carried the moonshine and placed it in the high grass beside the dogwood tree in the sideyard. Then I carried the whiskey bottle onto the carport. I opened a cage with a king snake in it and didn't even watch it disappear into the nearby stacks of books and newspapers. I tipped the bottle, watched the coral snake slide out of the bottle's neck into the cage. I carried the cage to the edge of the carport so that more of the glow from the streetlight would fall on the snake.

The coral snake was everything I had dreamed it would be, and much, much more. As beautiful as it had appeared in the photographs, I saw now how the camera had failed. The black, red, and yellow bands were a denser hue than any camera could capture. The small, delicate body gave the snake a grace of movement lacking in larger, bulkier snakes.

I lost all track of time and did not hear my father open and close the carport door. I was unaware of his presence until he crouched beside me and peered into the cage.

"That looks like a coral snake," he said in an alarmed voice as he picked up the cage for a better look.

"It's a scarlet king snake," I quickly lied.

"Are you sure?" my father said, still looking intently at the snake.

"I'm sure, Dad. Positive."

"But the bands are black, red, and yellow. I thought only coral snakes had those."

"Look," I said, trying to sound as convincing as possible, "scarlet king snakes have the same colors. Besides, coral snakes don't live this far west. You know that."

"That's true," my father said, putting the cage down. "Come on in," he said, standing up. "It's already past your bedtime."

I followed my father inside and waited in my darkened room three hours until my parents finally went to sleep. Then I sneaked into the kitchen, took the flashlight from the cupboard, and eased out the back door. I found the moonshine and walked up the street towards Bub Ely's. It was 11:30 according to my Mickey Mouse watch.

The lights were off at the Ely house, but there was enough of a moon that I did not need the flashlight to make my way to the garage. Once there, however, I did not lay the jar down in a corner. Instead, I unscrewed it. Everything that Badeye had put in my hands before had been magical. I wanted to know what magic the jar held. I pressed it to my lips, poured a mouthful. I held it there for a moment, and despite the kerosene taste, made a split-second decision to swallow instead of spit it out. When I did, I gagged, almost dropped the jar. My eyes teared. My throat and stomach burned. When the burning finally stopped, I placed the jar in a corner, walked slowly home.

I will never know for sure if what I did next would have happened had I not sampled Badeye's moonshine, but I did not go inside when I got home. Instead, I went to the carport to look at the coral snake, placing the flashlight against the cage for a better view. Finally, just looking wasn't good enough. I opened the cage and gently placed my right thumb and index finger behind the snake's head, but my hold was too far behind the head. The coral snake's mouth gripped my index finger.

I snatched my hand out of the cage, slung the snake from my finger, and screamed loud enough to be heard over the window fan in my parent's room. My scream was not one of pain but of knowledge. I knew the small, barely bleeding mark would not cause the agonizing swelling of a copperhead or rattlesnake bite. The coral snake's poison affected the nervous system, the heart. I also knew that four out of twenty people recently bitten by coral snakes in the Southeast had died. It was this knowledge that paralyzed me, made me unable to move, for my books had assured me the chances of a child's dying from a coral snake's bite were even greater.

And I very well might have died, if my father had not

been able to act in a focused manner. He ran out onto the carport in his underwear, took my trembling hands and asked what had happened. I pointed to the snake coiled on the concrete floor.

"It's a coral," I whimpered, and showed him the bite mark.

My mother was at the doorway in her nightgown, asking my father in a frantic voice what was the matter, though a part of her already knew.

"He's been bitten," my father said, walking rapidly towards my mother. "I've got to call the hospital, tell them they need to get antivenom rushed here from Charlotte."

My father was now on the carport steps. He turned to my mother. "Get him to the hospital. Quick. I'll get over there fast as I can."

My father brushed by my mother, who had not moved, only stood there looking at me. He brought her the car keys. "Go," he shouted, almost shoving her out onto the carport.

My mother saw the coral snake coiled on the concrete between us, but she did not hesitate. She stepped right over it and caught me as I collapsed into her arms.

The sound of rain pelting the windows woke me. I opened my eyes to whiteness, the unadorned walls of Cleveland County Hospital. My father and mother were sitting in metal chairs placed beside my bed. Their heads were bowed, and at first I thought they were asleep, but when I stirred they looked up, offered weary smiles.

Three days later I was released, and in a week I was feeling healthy enough to help my father fill my Uncle Earl's pickup truck with my snake collection. We first drove down to Broad River, taking the bumpy dirt road that followed the river until we were several miles from the nearest house. We opened the cages, watched the contents slither away.

Then we drove back towards home, stopping a mile from Cliffside at the town dump. My father backed the truck up to the edge of the landfill and we lowered the tailgate. We threw the snake-and-alcohol-filled jars out of the truck, watched them shatter against the ground, and knew they would soon be buried forever under tons of other things people no longer wanted.

As for Badeye, I ignored his offers of free snowcones. My parents ignored his apologies. After several attempts at reconciliation failed, Badeye stopped slowing down as he approached our house, even sped up a little as his truck glided past into the twilight.

That October Badeye left Cliffside. When he pulled into Heddon's Gulf station, his possessions piled into the back of his truck, Charlie Heddon asked him where he was moving to. Badeye only shrugged his shoulders and muttered, "Somewhere where it's warmer." No one ever saw him again.

I remember my mother staring out the kitchen window that autumn as the dogwood tree began to shed its leaves. It would not be until years later that I would understand how wonderful those falling leaves made her feel, for they signaled summer's end and the coming cold weather, the first frost that would banish snakes (including the coral snake which we never found), as well as Badeye and his snowcones. But I also remember the first bite of my first snowcone that June evening when Badeye suddenly appeared on our street. Nothing else has ever tasted so good.

: Tracy :

The Night the New Jesus Fell to Earth

The day after it happened, and Cliffside's new Jesus and my old husband was in the county hospital in fair but stable condition, Preacher Thompson, claiming it was all his fault, offered his resignation to the board of deacons. But he wasn't to blame. He'd only been here a couple of months, fresh out of preacher's college, and had probably never had to deal with a snake like Larry Rudisell before. A man or a woman, as I've found out the hard way, usually has to get bit by a snake before they start watching out for them.

What I mean is, Preacher Thompson's intentions were good. At his very first interview the pulpit committee had told him what a sorry turn our church had taken in the last few years, and they hadn't left out much either. They told him about Len Deaton, our former choir director, who left his choir, wife, and eight children to run off to Florida with a singer at Harley's Lounge who wasn't even a Baptist. And they told about Preacher Crowe, who had gotten so senile he had preached the same sermon four weeks in a row, though they didn't mention that a lot of the congregation hadn't even noticed. The committee told him about how membership had been slipping for several years, how the church was in a rut, and how when Preacher Crowe had finally retired in November, it had been clear that some major changes had to be made if the church was going to survive. And this was exactly why they wanted him to be the new minister, they told him. He was young and energetic and could bring some fresh blood into the church and help get it going in the right direction. Which was exactly what he tried to do, and exactly why Larry was able to talk his way onto that cross.

It did take a few weeks, though. At first Preacher Thompson was so nervous when he preached that I expected him to bolt for the sanctuary door at any moment. He wouldn't even look up from his notes, and when he performed his first baptism he almost drowned poor little Eddie Gregory by holding him under the water too long. Still, each week you could see him get a little more comfortable and confident, and by the last Sunday in February, about two months ago, he gave the sermon everybody had been waiting for. It was all about commitment and the need for new ideas, about how a church was like a car, and our church was in reverse and we had to get it back in forward. You could tell he was really working himself up because he wasn't looking at his notes or his watch. It was 12:15, the first time he'd ever kept us up after twelve, when he closed, telling us that Easter, a month away, was a time of rebirth, and he wanted us all to go home and think of some way our church could be reborn too, something that would get Cliffside Baptist Church back in the right gear.

Later I wondered if maybe all the car talk had something to do with what happened, because the next Sunday Preacher Thompson announced he'd gotten many good suggestions, but there was one in particular that was truly inspired, one that could truly put the church back on the right road, and he wanted the man who had come up with the idea, Larry Rudisell, to stand up and tell the rest of the congregation about it.

Like I said earlier, once you've been bitten by a snake you start looking out for them, but there's something else too. You start to know their ways. So I knew right off that whatever Larry was about to unfold, he was expecting to get something out of it, because having been married to this snake for almost three years, I knew him better than he knew himself. Larry's a hustler. Always has been. He came out of his momma talking out of both sides of his mouth, trying to hustle her, the nurse, the doctor, whichever one he saw first. He hasn't stopped talking or hustling since.

Larry stood up, wearing a sport coat he couldn't button because of his beer gut, no tie, and enough gold around his neck to fill every tooth in Cleveland County. He was also wearing his sincere "I'd swear on my dead momma's grave I didn't know that odometer had been turned back" look, which was as phony as the curls in his brillo-pad hairdo, which he'd done that way to cover up his bald spot.

Then Larry started telling about what he was calling his "vision," claiming that late Friday night he'd woke up, half blinded by bright flashing lights and hearing a voice coming out of the ceiling, telling him to recreate the crucifixion on the front lawn of Cliffside Baptist Church, at night, with lights shining on the three men on the crosses. The whole thing sounded more like one of those U.F.O. stories in *The National Examiner* than a religious experience, and about as believable. Larry looked around and started telling how he just knew people would come from miles away to see it, just like they went to McAdenville every December to see the Christmas lights, and then he said he believed in his vision enough to pay for it himself.

Then Larry stopped to see if his sales pitch was working. He was selling his crucifixion idea the same way he would sell a '84 Buick in his car lot. And it was working. Larry has always been a smooth talker. He talked me into the back seat of his daddy's car when I was seventeen, talked me into marrying him when I was eighteen, and talked me out of divorcing him on the grounds of adultery a half dozen times. I finally got smart and plugged up my ears with cotton so I couldn't hear him while I packed my belongings.

Larry started talking again, telling the congregation he didn't want to take any credit for the idea, that he was just a messenger and that the last thing God had told him was that he wanted Larry to play Jesus, and his mechanic, Terry Wooten, to play one of the thieves, a role, as far as I was concerned, Terry had been playing as long as he'd worked for Larry. When I looked over at Terry, the expression on his face made it quite clear that God hadn't bothered to contact him about all of this. Then I looked up at the ceiling to see if it was about to collapse and bury us all. Everybody was quiet for about five seconds. Then the whole congregation started talking at once, and it sounded more like a tobacco auction than a church service.

After a couple of minutes people remembered where they were, and it got a little more civilized. At least they were raising their hands and getting acknowledged before they started shouting. The first to speak was Jimmy Wells, who had once bought an Olds 88 from Larry and had the transmission fall out not a half-mile from where he had driven it off Larry's lot. Jimmy was still bitter about that, so I wasn't too surprised when he nominated his brother-in-law Harry Bayne to play Jesus.

As soon as Jimmy sat down, Larry popped up like a jack-in-the-box, claiming Harry couldn't play Jesus because Harry had a glass eye. When Jimmy asked why that mattered, Larry said they didn't have glass eyes back in olden times and Jimmy said nobody would notice and Larry said yes they would because the color in Harry's real eye was different than in the glass eye. Jimmy and Larry kept arguing. Harry finally got up and said if it meant that much to Larry to let him do it, that he was too hungry to care anymore.

Preacher Thompson had pretty much stayed out of all this till Harry said that, but then he suggested that Harry play the thief who gets saved, leaving Terry as the other one. The Splawn brothers, Donnie and Robbie, were nominated to be the Roman soldiers. To the credit of the church, when Preacher Thompson asked for a show of hands as to whether we should let this be our Easter project, it was close. My hand wasn't the only one that went up against it, and I still believe it was empty stomachs as much as a belief in Larry and his scheme that got it passed.

But it did pass, and a few days later Preacher Thompson called me up and asked, since I was on the church's building and grounds committee, if I would help build the crosses. You see, I'm a carpenter, the only full-time one, male or female, in the church, so whenever the church's softball field needs a new backstop or the parsonage needs some repair work, I'm the one who usually does it. And I do it right. Carpentry is in my blood. People around here say my father was the best carpenter to ever drive a nail in western North Carolina, and after my mother died when I was nine, he would take me with him every day I wasn't in school. By the time I was fourteen, I was working full-time with him in the summers. I quit school when I was sixteen. I knew how I wanted to make my living. I've been a carpenter for the last fifteen years.

It was hard at first. Since I was a woman, a lot of men didn't think I could do as good a job as they could. But one good thing about being a carpenter is someone can look at your work and know right away if you know what you're doing. Nowadays, my reputation as a carpenter is as good as any man's in the county.

Still, I was a little surprised that Preacher Thompson asked me to work on a project my ex-husband was so involved in. But, being new, he might not have known we had once been married. I do go by my family's name now. Or maybe he did know, figuring since the divorce was over five years ago we had forgiven each other like

Christians should. Despite its being Larry's idea, I did feel obligated since I was on the building and grounds committee, so I said I would help. Preacher Thompson thanked me and said we would meet in front of the church at ten on Saturday morning.

On Saturday, me, Preacher Thompson, Larry, and Ed Watt, who's an electrician, met on the front lawn. From the very start, it was obvious Larry was going to run the show, telling us the way everything should be, pointing and waving his arms like he was a Hollywood director. He had on a white, ruffled shirt that was open to his gut, his half-ton of gold necklaces, and a pair of sunglasses. Larry was not just trying to act like but look like he was from California, which meant, as far as I was concerned, that, unlike Jesus, he actually deserved to be nailed to a cross.

Larry showed me where he wanted the three crosses, and he gave me the length he wanted them. His was supposed to be three feet taller than the other two. Preacher Thompson was close by, so we acted civil to one another till I walked over to my truck to go get the wood I'd need. Larry followed me, and as soon as I got in the truck and cranked it, he asked me how it felt to have only a pillow to hold every night. "Lot of advantages to it," I said as I drove off. "A pillow don't snore and it don't have inch-long toenails and it don't smell like a brewery." I was already out of shouting distance before he could think of anything to say to that.

I was back an hour later with three eight-inch-thick poles, just like the ones I used to build the backstop for the softball field, and a railroad crosstie I'd sawed into three lengthwise pieces for the part the arms would be stretched out on. I'd also gotten three blocks of wood I was going to put where their feet would be to take the strain off their arms.

As I turned into the church parking lot, I saw that Wanda Wilson's LTD was parked in the back of the church. She was out by the car with Larry, wearing a pink sweatshirt and a pair of blue running shorts, even though it was barely 60 degrees, just to show off her legs. When they saw me they started kissing and putting their hands all over each other. They kept that up for a good five minutes, in clear view of not just me but Ed Watt and Preacher Thompson too, and I thought we were going to have to get a water hose and spray them, the same way you would two dogs, to get them apart.

Finally, Wanda got into her LTD and left, maybe to get a cold shower, and Larry came over to the truck. As soon as he saw the poles in the back of the truck he got all worked up, saying they were too big around, that they looked like telephone poles, that he was supposed to be Jesus, not the Wichita Lineman. That was enough for me. I put my toolbox back in the cab and told Preacher Thompson Benny Brown was coming over with his post-hole digger around noon. I pointed at Larry. "I forgot all about Jesus being a carpenter," I said. "I'm taking all of this back over to Hamrick's Lumberyard." Then I drove off and didn't look back.

Why is it that some men always have to act like they know more than another human being just because that other human being happens to be a woman? Larry's never driven a nail in his life, but he couldn't admit that I would know what would make the best and safest cross. I guess some people never change. Ever since the divorce was made final, Larry has gone out of his way to be as ugly as possible to me. The worst thing about being divorced in a small town is that you're always running into your ex. Sometimes it seems I see him more now than I did when I was married to him. I can live with that.

But it's been a lot harder to live with the lies he's been spreading around town, claiming things about me that involved whips and dog collars and Black Sabbath albums. You'd think nobody would believe such things, but like the Bible says, it's a fallen world. A lot of people want to believe the worst, so a lot of them believed Larry when he started spreading his lies. I couldn't get a date for almost two years, and I lost several girlfriends too. Like the song says, "Her hands are callused but her heart is tender." That rumor caused me more heartache than you could believe.

I have no idea what they did after I drove off that Saturday, but the Sunday before Easter the crosses were up, so after church let out just about everybody in the congregation went out on the front lawn to get a better look. I've always said you can tell a lot about a person by how carefully they build something or put something together, but looking at Larry's crosses didn't tell me a thing I didn't already know. Instead of using a pole for the main section, he had gotten four-by-eight boards made out of cedar, which anybody who knows anything about wood can tell you is the weakest wood you can buy. The crossties and footrests were the same. I'm not even going to mention how sorry the nailing was.

I walked over to the middle cross, gave it a push, and felt it give like a popsicle stick in sand. I kneeled beside it and dug up enough dirt to see they hadn't put any cement in the hole Benny Brown had dug for them but had just packed dirt in it. I got up and walked over to the nearest spigot and washed the red dirt off my hands while everybody watched me, waiting for me to pass judgment on Larry's crosses. "All I'm going to say is this," I said as I finished drying my hands. "Anybody who gets up on one of those things had better have a whole lot of faith."

Of course Larry wasn't going to let me have the last word. He started saying I was just jealous that he'd done such a good job, that I didn't know the difference between a telephone pole and a cross. I didn't say another word, but as I was walking to my truck I heard Harry Bayne tell Larry he was going to have to find somebody else to play his role, that he'd rather find a safer way to prove his faith, like maybe handling a rattlesnake or drinking strychnine. I went back that night to look at the crosses some more. I left convinced more than ever that the crosses, especially the taller middle one, wouldn't support the weight of a full-grown man.

On Good Friday I went on over to the church about an hour before they were scheduled to start, mainly because I didn't believe they would be able to get up there without at least one of the crosses snapping like a piece of dry kindling. There were already a good number of people there, including Larry's cousin Kevin, who wasn't a member of our church or anybody else's, but who worked part-time for Larry and was enough like Larry to be a good salesman and a pitiful excuse for a human being. Kevin was spitting tobacco juice into a paper cup while Mrs. Murrel, who used to teach drama over at the high school, dabbed red paint on his face and hands and feet, trying to make him look like the crucified thief Larry had talked, paid, or threatened him into playing. Besides the paint, the only thing he was wearing was a sweatshirt with a picture of Elvis on it and what looked like a giant diaper, though I'd already heard the preacher explain to several people it was supposed to be what the Bible called a loincloth. Terry Wooten was standing over by the crosses, dressed up the same way, looking like he was about to vomit as he stared up at where he would be hanging in only a few more minutes.

Then I saw the sign and suddenly everything that had been going on for the last month made sense. It was one of those portable electric ones with about a hundred colored light bulbs bordering it. "The Crucifixion of JESUS CHRIST Is Paid for and Presented by LARRY RUDISELL'S Used Cars of Cliffside, North Carolina" was spelled out in red plastic letters at the top of the message board. Near the bottom in green letters it said, "If JESUS Had Driven A Car, He Would Have Bought It At LARRY'S." It was the tackiest, most sacrilegious thing I'd ever seen in my life.

Finally, the new Jesus himself appeared, coming out of the church with what looked like a brown, rotting halo on his head—it was his crown of thorns—fifty yards of extension cord covering his shoulder, and a cigarette hanging out of his mouth. He unrolled the cord as he came across the lawn, dressed like Kevin and Terry except he didn't have any red paint on his face. Larry didn't have a fake beard either. He wanted everyone to know it was Larry Rudisell up on that cross. He walked over to the sign and plugged the extension cord into it.

You know what it's like when the flashbulb goes off when you're getting a picture taken and you stagger around half blind for a while? Well, that's about the effect Larry's sign had when it came on. The colored lights were flashing on and off, and you could have seen it from a mile away. Larry watched for a minute to make sure it was working right and then announced it was twenty minutes to show time so they needed to go ahead and get up on the crosses. Preacher Thompson and the Splawn brothers went and got the stepladders and brought them over to where the crosses were. Terry and Kevin slinked over behind the sign, trying to hide. It was obvious Larry was going to have to get up there first.

Larry took off his sweatshirt, and I realized for the first time they were going to go up there with nothing except the bedsheets wrapped around them. It wasn't that cold right then, but like it always is in March, it was windy. I knew that in a few minutes, when the sun went down, the temperature would really fall fast.

While Donnie and Robbie Splawn steadied the cross, Larry crawled up the ladder. With only the loincloth wrapped around him, he looked more like a Japanese Sumo wrestler on *Wide World of Sports* than Jesus. When he got far enough up, Larry reached over, grabbed the crosstie, and put his feet on the board he was going to stand on. He turned himself around until he faced us. I'll never know how the cross held, but it did.

It was completely dark, except of course for Larry's sign, by the time Terry and Kevin had been placed on their crosses. As I watched I couldn't help thinking that if they ever did want to bring back crucifixion, the three hanging up there in the dark would be as good a bunch to start with as any. I looked over my shoulder and saw the traffic was already piled up, and the whole front lawn was filled with people. There was even a TV crew from WSOC in Charlotte.

At 6:30 the music began, and the spotlights Ed Watt had rigged up came on. I had to admit it was impressive, especially if you were far enough away so you didn't see Larry's stomach or Terry's chattering teeth. The WSOC cameras were rolling, and more and more people were crowding onto the lawn and even spilling out into the road, making the first traffic jam in Cliffside's history even worse.

The crucifixion was supposed to last an hour, but after twenty minutes the wind started to pick up, and the crosses began making creaking noises, moving back and forth a little more with each gust of wind. It wasn't long before Terry began to make some noises too, screaming over the music for someone to get a ladder and get him down. I didn't blame him. The crosses were really starting to sway, and Terry, Kevin, and Larry looked like acrobats in some circus high-wire act. But there wasn't a net for them to land in if they fell.

Preacher Thompson and Ed Watt were running to get the ladders, but at least for Larry, it was too late. His cross swung forward one last time, and then I heard the sound of wood cracking. Donnie Splawn heard it too, and he tripped on his Roman Soldier's robe as he ran to get out of the way. Larry screamed out "God help me," probably the sincerest prayer of his life. But it went unanswered. The crosses began to fall forward, and Larry, with his arms outstretched, looked like a man doing a swan dive. I closed my eyes at the last second but heard him hit.

Then everything was chaos. People were screaming and shouting and running around in all directions. Janice Hamrick, who's a registered nurse, came out of the crowd to tend to Larry till the rescue squad could get there and take him to the county hospital. Several other people ran over to stabilize the other two crosses. When Terry saw what happened to his boss, he stained his loincloth. His eyes were closed, and he was praying so fast only God could understand what he was saying. Kevin wasn't saying or doing anything because he had fainted dead away the second his cousin hit the ground.

It's been three weeks now since all this happened. Larry got to leave the county hospital, miraculously, alive, on Easter morning, but his jaw is still wired shut, and it's going to stay that way for at least another month. But despite the broken jaw and broken nose, he still goes out to his car lot every day. Since people over half the state saw him hit the ground, in slow motion, on WSOC's six o'clock news, Larry's become western North Carolina's leading tourist attraction. They come from more miles away than you would believe just to see him, and then he gets his pad and pencil out and tries to sell them a car. Quite a few times he does. As a matter of fact, I hear he's sold more cars in the last two weeks than any two-week period in his life, which is further proof that, as the Bible tells us, we live in a fallen world.

Still, some good things have happened. When Preacher Thompson offered to resign, the congregation made it clear they wanted him to stay, and he has. But he's toned down his sermons a good bit, and last Sunday, when Larry handed him a proposal for an outdoor manger scene with you know who playing Joseph, Preacher Thompson just crumpled it up and threw it in the trashcan.

As for me, a lot of people remember that I was the one who said the crosses were unsafe in the first place, especially one person, Harry Bayne. Two weeks ago Harry took me out to eat as a way of saying thank you. We hit it off and have spent a lot of time together lately. We're going dancing over at Harley's Lounge tonight. I'm still a little scared, almost afraid to hope for too much, but I'm beginning to believe than even in a fallen world things can sometimes look up.

Love and Pain

Darlene walks through the open sliding door dragging two trees worth of divorce papers. Lord, she is beautiful, even as she harps on me about keeping the door open while the air conditioner is running in the other room. Darlene and her lawyer are setting me up where I won't have an extra dime for the next five hundred years, and she's telling me I need to watch my power bill. I follow her into the den, wishing I had a pair of blinders like they put on mules. Seeing her again after two months is killing me. It's like trying to give up smoking and someone putting a lighted cigarette in your hand.

I look out the window and see Carl Blowmeyer in his backyard, barbecuing what looks like a large dog and looking this way. Blowmeyer is one of millions of northern retirees who have moved down here to live cheaper and to educate us southerners about how to drive on snow. The one or two times each year the white stuff falls, Blowmeyer stands on main street with a Mr. Microphone and tells drivers what they're doing wrong.

Spring and summer mornings he's out in the yard with his lawnmower, weedeater, and electric hedge clippers. Blowmeyer's grass is cut shorter than most golf course greens. He crawls around his yard on hands and knees to find wild onions and crabgrass. Now Blowmeyer is stretching his neck to see over the hedge, wanting to watch every minute of the soap opera next door. His shorter, grub-white wife stands in the lawn chair. They love my pain.

Darlene pushes empty Dos Equis bottles to the edge of the coffee table so she can spread out the divorce papers. She looks at the bottles and shakes her head. Darlene's never had a drink in her life, and she used to punish me for my weakness by buying the cheapest beer she could find.

"That beer is six dollars a six pack," she says.

"I bought it to help out the Mexicans," I say. "They're in bad shape down there."

"Read and sign," she says. "Stanley's expecting me back at nine."

I read. She will get the house, the car, and most of the five thousand in the bank. As far as I can tell, I get the pickup and all the food in the refrigerator.

I finish reading but I don't look up. I'm thinking about the day we got married and how she looked right into my eyes and swore all that stuff about for better or for worse and for richer or for poorer. And now all those words, all those promises, have come to this.

"I loved you," I say. "I think I might still. I didn't mean to kill the monkey. I'd swear on a Bible I didn't." Once I start talking I can't stop. I sound like the worst drunk you ever sat next to in a bar.

I am a little drunk. If I'd been sober as a cow I'd have said the same thing—except I wouldn't have said it.

"I wanted a child," Darlene says. "You wouldn't give me a child. You gave me a monkey and then you killed it."

"Couldn't," I say. "Couldn't. The doctors said it happens sometimes. It's nothing a man can help."

"Stanley says you could help it. He says you didn't want a child, so your mind told your body to kill all those sperm. It's psychological, something you wouldn't understand. And then you killed Little Napoleon. Stanley says Little Napoleon was our symbolic child, and you killed him because you hated him. Stanley knows what he's talking about. His minor at Auburn was psychology."

I pick up the pen and begin to sign. I'm too much of a Baptist not to believe I'm guilty, even when I'm not exactly sure what I'm guilty of. Darlene is at least partly right. I had hated the monkey. Buying it had been a big mistake, but things had gotten so tense by then I felt I had nothing to lose. She had said she needed something else to love, something more than me. I couldn't give her a child, so I drove to Charlotte. A spider monkey was the closest thing I could find.

She had loved the monkey, and at first even loved me again. It was the Indian summer of our marriage. We were like a family. Every Friday after supper we would go to Greene's Cafe and eat banana splits, then drive over to Shelby and play putt-putt, just like any other family. I tried my best. I even went with Darlene and Little Napoleon to Stanley's office for his shots and checkups. But the monkey hated me from the very beginning. At night if I got up to go to the bathroom, it would wait till I started making water, then come flying out of the darkness, grab a calf, and draw blood. It got so bad I just stayed in bed and held it. Now I have chronic bladder problems.

Yes, I hated the little bastard, but I didn't kill it on purpose. How could I know it had crawled into the washing machine when I went to the pantry to get the Tide. It was probably hiding in the bottom, waiting for me to stick my hand in so it could bite me again.

The marriage was as good as over by the rinse cycle. Darlene took the corpse to Stanley's office. He is part owner of the pet cemetery, so he arranged the funeral service and the burial. I wasn't allowed to attend. Then Darlene started what she called "grief therapy" with Stanley, the only veterinarian/psychologist in western North Carolina. After the first week Darlene became a vegetarian. "Animals have souls," she had said. "To eat one is a barbaric act."

"What about plants," I had asked. "If animals have souls, why not plants? Where do you draw the line?"

"That's exactly the kind of thing Stanley said you would say," she had said.

Three weeks later she moved in with Stanley.

I finish signing the papers. "As soon as this divorce is final," Darlene says, "Stanley and I are getting married." She gathers the papers together.

"It's not too late to give us another try," I say.

"Yes, it is," she says, already bored with the conversation.

"I tried to make you happy. I gave up the farm. I wore a tie and worked with jerks so we could afford this house."

"The farm was going broke," Darlene says. "You would have been bankrupt in another two years. You'll have to do better than that."

"I quit chewing tobacco and started listening to Public Radio. I increased my vocabulary. I tried not to act like a redneck."

"And failed," she says.

"I tried to give you a baby. I suffered indignities. I filled dixie cups with semen in strange doctors' offices."

"I suffered indignities too," Darlene says. "And it wasn't even my problem."

"I loved you," I say and there's enough truth in that to make her look away, at least for a moment.

"I'll prove it," I say. "I'll change. I'll quit drinking, become a vegetarian."

"You can't change enough," she says, taking the documents off the coffee table.

"I'll be friendly to the neighbors. Invite them over to eat salads. I'll make the salads myself."

"Not enough," Darlene says, standing up.

"I'll buy you a new monkey and I will love it."

"Not enough," she says, walking out of the den. "No other monkey could ever replace Little Napoleon."

"I'll walk over hot coals. I'll watch whales."

"Not enough," she says from the kitchen.

I hear her car engine and remember one other thing. I hurry through the kitchen. I'm almost outside when I smash against nothing. Then the whole world shatters around me. I fall out on the pavement. Pieces of glass cover my body. I'm bleeding in a hundred places.

Darlene's headlights are shining on me. I slowly stand up, pulling glass from my skin. Darlene rolls down her window and shouts over the engine. "Not enough," she says, and drives off.

Blowmeyer runs over with a barbecue fork in his hand, the albino gasping to keep up.

"She shot him," he tells his wife. "Five or six times."

Blowmeyer is so excited he has spilled barbecue sauce on his pants.

"Go get the movie camera, Lorraine," he tells his wife. "And call the rescue squad."

The albino disappears. I ignore Blowmeyer. I lie down on the grass, close my eyes and feel pain cut through the alcohol and the nest of spiders scrambling around inside my head, that other kind of pain, the worst kind.

I don't open my eyes until I hear the rescue squad wail into the driveway, almost hitting Blowmeyer who is filming it all.

"Save me a copy," I tell Blowmeyer as the attendants take my arms and walk me to the back of the ambulance. "I'm O.K.," I keep telling them, wanting to believe it. "I'm fine."

II

Yard of the Month

I was twelve years old when one late June Sunday my family came home from church and did not eat fried chicken, green beans, rice and gravy, homemade rolls, and banana pudding. Instead, my mother opened up a can of Spam, placed it on a paper plate with some saltine crackers, poured two glasses of warm tea, and without saying a word left my father and me for the solitude of her bedroom.

I sat in my chair staring at the Spam and crackers, too stunned to move or speak. Over the years, our Sunday dinner had become a religious rite, a ritualistic ending to a morning of Sunday School and preaching. Such a view was due in large part to conversations with my sole Catholic classmate, Raymond Von Drelle, who told of eating crackers and drinking wine at each church service. I had come to see fried chicken, green beans, rice and gravy, homemade rolls, and banana pudding as a Southern Baptist equivalent to the Roman Catholic Communion. My mother's Sunday dinner of Spam and crackers bordered on blasphemy.

My father, however, seemed unaware anything had changed. He had already begun to eat the Spam and crackers as he stared out the window toward the dogwood tree in the sideyard. That my father had not noticed any change in our family's routine did not surprise me, for my mother had taught me the facts of life years earlier. By facts of life I do not mean knowledge about sex. Like most good Baptists, my mother knew I would learn about that subject in snickering conversations with my classmates. The facts of life, at least in the Hampton household, concerned my father's bizarre behavior, though bizarre may have been too strong a word, for my father had not, like Dooley Ross, chosen to live in a fall-out shelter, or, like our next-door neighbor Lulu Hawkins, claimed to have grown a head of cabbage with the face of Jesus on it and then mailed the cabbage, packed in ice, to Billy Graham. My father, as my mother put it, was "different."

The most obvious difference was his job. Unlike most of the townspeople and all our relatives, my father did not farm or work in one of the county's five textile mills. He taught art at the junior college just outside of town. But there was also a difference in temperament. Over the years Cliffside's citizens had had enough contact with the college's professors to realize almost all of them were eccentric, but, perhaps because he was also an artist, my father's behavior was always a little more unusual than that of his colleagues. Everyone in town knew the story of how he had once taught a full day of classes in his bedroom slippers. They knew he would order lunch uptown at Greene's Cafe, start reading an art book, completely forget about his meal, and go back to the college without touching his food.

My mother and I had witnessed similar behavior time

and time again. We knew, for instance, anytime my father was driving there was a good chance he would drive right by our destination if my mother and I did not keep a constant vigil. If a lightbulb burned out, he just got up and went to another room to read. She and I knew he could not care less if the roof was leaking, the leaves needed raking, or the grass needed cutting.

I had always assumed that my mother, though irritated at times by my father's behavior—as when she turned on a light switch and nothing happened or when she had to call her seventy-year-old uncle to come over with his bushhog and mow the jungle in our front yard—had viewed my father's actions with the same good-natured humor as the townspeople. That his behavior might have embarrassed and even humiliated her had never crossed my mind. But when I got up from the table where my father continued to eat and walked in the darkened bedroom where my mother lay on the bed, I found out otherwise.

When I asked what was wrong, she raised her head from the damp pillow.

"I thought I could stand it, but I can't anymore," she said and lay her face back down on the pillow. What my mother could not stand was the humiliation of being married to a man unconcerned with the outward appearance of his home. Between muffled sobs my mother confessed she had never joined the Cliffside Garden Club or the junior college's Faculty Wives Auxiliary because she knew the time would come when the monthly meeting would be held at our house. The thought of her guests wading through the front yard's knee-high grass and then winding their way through the labyrinth of pottery, books, old news-papers, and other debris that filled our carport was too much for my mother.

"Even Dr. Moseby," my mother said bitterly, speaking of the college's chemistry professor who had once intro-duced his wife by the wrong first name at the college ban-quet, "even he keeps his yard up. Do you realize, son, that the back and side yards have never been cut since we moved into this house fifteen years ago?" My mother's voice softened for a moment. "It must be hard on you too," she said. My mother attempted a sympathetic smile. "I know your father must be a constant embarrassment to you."

I nodded in agreement, more to make my mother be-lieve she was not alone than in any real suffering on my part. Like my classmate Harry Bayne, whose father had a metal plate in his head, I was still at an age I could be proud of my father's abnormalities.

My mother continued talking, and I soon found out why, after years of accepting her fate, her fortitude had crumbled this particular Sunday. Because my father had spilled black-berry jam on his white dress shirt at breakfast and my mother had not noticed until we were in the car, we had been late to Sunday School that morning. She was about to enter the classroom when she heard our family men-tioned by Mrs. Ely, the president of the Cliffside Garden Club. Mrs. Ely's husband had died two years earlier (the one thing in thirty years of marriage, at least according to my Uncle Earl, he had done without his wife's permis-sion). One month after his death, she had founded the Cliffside Garden Club and then dared anyone not to vote for her as president. What my mother overheard Mrs. Ely saying was that in the last ten years only two homes, ours and Dooley Ross's, had not had the Cliffside Garden Club's "Yard of the Month" plaque placed on a metal stake in their front yards. "Dooley Ross has an excuse," Mrs. Ely had said. "He doesn't have a wife. A man left alone will live like a hog. When women want to live that way too, the world is in sad shape." Now whether Dooley Ross's fallout shelter was (a)really a home or (b)had a yard (the only grass growing was on the roof.) were questions I might have raised at some other time, but I sensed this was not the moment to bring these matters up.

"I just want our family," my mother said with a weary sigh, "to be like everyone else's just once, just to see what it feels like."

I left the bedroom and found my father, having finished his Spam and crackers, in the living room reading a book on Leonardo Da Vinci. I knew from experience it was almost impossible to talk to him while he was reading. You could talk at him, as my mother often did, but his usual reply was either a grunt or, if she were especially insistent, an "all right," an all-purpose phrase that could answer almost any question my mother could ask, from "Do you want to eat at 6:30?" to "James, the house is on fire!" without his having to look up from his book. I knew drastic measures were necessary. Driven by my mother's tears, I went up to my father and slowly but firmly took the book out of his hand. He looked up at me in astonishment.

"We've got to talk, Dad," I said, holding Leonardo in my hand as a hostage for negotiations. My father looked up at me and, at least for the moment, I had his full attention.

"Mom's upset," I said. "She's crying." I spent the next five minutes explaining why, and though my father cast several longing glances at the book I clinched in my hand, he was listening. When I finished, he spoke.

"I'll call your Uncle Earl to come over with his bushhog. I'll get him to do the backyard too."

"That's not enough," I said. "That isn't going to get us yard of the month."

"I see," he said. "Well, I'll have to think a while on what to do." He frowned slightly. "Did you say your mother was crying?"

When I nodded, he left me and the biography of Leonardo and disappeared into the bedroom. He and my mother stayed in their bedroom a long time, almost an hour. When my mother came out her eyes were red, but she was no longer crying. I assumed my father had made some undying vow of love and, more importantly, had promised to make our yard presentable.

The next morning, as soon as he finished teaching his summer school class, my father came into my bedroom and told me to get into the car, that we had a lot to do. I put down the *Mad* magazine I was reading and followed him out. He did not explain where we were going, but in a couple of minutes we were walking into Hamrick's Hardware. Until that moment, I had believed my father was unaware Hamrick's Hardware even existed. Whenever something broke down in our home, either one of my mother's relatives or Bob Burrus, the town handyman, repaired it. The liver-spotted old men who spent a good portion of their waking hours in the store, lying a lot and buying very little, quit talking as soon as we walked in, no doubt because of the historical nature of my father's first visit. Cecil Hamrick must have yearned for years in his hardware heart for this moment, for he almost tripped over a merry tiller getting to my father before he could get away. Of course, my father had made no list, but to my surprise he seemed to know what was needed. With a little assistance from Cecil, we soon managed to block the front of the store with the first lawn mower in the Hampton family history, a gasoline can, a sling blade, lawn clippers, a rake, a pick sheet, and two pairs of work gloves. The bill came to $98.43. Cecil gave us two caps with "Hamrick's Hardware" printed on the front. He knew great advertising when he saw it.

After we stopped at the Gulf station to fill up the gas can, we drove on home and unloaded our purchases as my mother watched from the kitchen window. My father put on his "Hamrick's Hardware" hat and filled the mower with gas. Then he slowly looked over the yard, truly seeing it, I was convinced, for the first time in his life. Because the front yard had been bushhogged by Uncle Earl in May, it could be handled with just the mower, but the sling blade would have to be used in the side and back yards before a lawn mower could go more than a foot or two without stalling. My father put on his work gloves and picked up the sling blade. I was given the other pair of gloves and the clippers and told to trim around the edge of the house.

Although only mid-morning, it was already hot and humid. My father had either forgotten or felt it unnecessary to change his clothes, and after another fifteen minutes of slinging briars and kudzu in the side yard, his blue dress shirt was stained with sweat, his gray dress pants covered with beggar's lice. Nevertheless, as amusing as he looked in his "Hamrick's Hardware" cap and professor's clothes, one thing was obvious—he had used a sling blade before. His stroke was smooth and economical as he slashed through the belt-high jungle. Watching him swing the sling blade was like watching Roberto Clemente swing a baseball bat. There was no wasted effort or energy. In less than an hour he had not only chased two rabbits and a five-foot-long king snake out of the side yard but had also cut the kudzu, briars, and weeds to a length a mower could manage.

Meanwhile, I had finished trimming one side of the house without losing any fingers, but despite the gloves, blisters were already forming on my palms. My father came over to where I was working and took a moment to catch his breath and wipe his brow with his shirtsleeve before he spoke.

"I'm going to sling the back," he said, "and when I finish I want you to walk through the grass and pick up anything that might get caught in the mower, O.K.?"

He smiled and put his arm around me, an action so out of character that I could only stand there speechless and sweating until he took his arm away and walked around to the backyard.

At noon my mother brought out tomato sandwiches and iced tea. We ate in the shade of the dogwood tree, my father gulping down tea by the glassful. He was covered with sweat, beggarlice, and bits of grass. His glasses continued to fog over with perspiration no matter how many times he wiped them with the small portions of his shirt that were not soaking wet. As soon as we finished our sandwiches, my mother told us to come inside because it was too hot to work, that we could finish tomorrow, a real risk on her part, for she knew as well as I did that once my father stopped he might never pick up the equipment again. But it was not like my father to stop any project before it was completed. It was not unusual for him to disappear into the basement of the art department for twelve hours at a time when he was throwing pots or painting, or to read a book of several hundred pages in one day. So neither my mother nor I was surprised when he put his cap back on and headed for the backyard. It was obvious he was going to finish the yard or die of sunstroke.

By two o'clock my father and his slingblade had destroyed the last wildlife sanctuary inside the Cliffside city limits, and I had finished trimming around the house. After drinking a quart of iced tea my mother had left near the carport, he asked me to pick up and put outside the carport anything that might get caught in the mower. I went out to the sideyard and began to make a search through the fallen briars and kudzu that was part Easter egg hunt and part archaeological dig. I had walked less than ten feet when I stumbled over a rusting Schwinn bicycle I had received for my sixth birthday. After carrying the bike up to the carport, I continued my search. In the next hour, as my father cut the front yard, I found an alarm clock, a one-armed teddy bear, six rotting newspapers with rubber bands still around them, a skeleton of a large (non-human) mammal, a hot-water bottle, a blue hula hoop, a hubcap, over a dozen soft drink bottles, two baseballs, and an unopened can of Luck's Blackeyed Peas.

By the time I had dragged these items up to the carport, my father had only half the backyard left to mow. I was exhausted and thirsty. As I went inside to get something to drink, Beverly Hedrick, one of my classmates, and her family drove slowly by our house, evidently out for a Sunday drive. I waved and thought nothing more of it, too weary even to remember that today was Monday, not Sunday.

When my mother saw how tired I was, she made me stay inside the rest of the afternoon. I could only listen as my father finished the backyard and then drove away in the Plymouth without saying a word to my mother. My mother did not say anything as we waited for his return, but I could tell that she was worried he might never come back, that he might drive all the way to Greenwich Village and join the bohemians who lived in one-room flats and never had to worry about mowing lawns or cleaning up carports.

But he did return, not in the Plymouth but in my Uncle Earl's pickup. By this time my mother and I had eaten supper, but my father did not stop to eat. Instead, he filled the back of the pickup with the artifacts of the Hampton civilization I had found and the books, magazines, and newspapers that clogged our carport. When the truck was filled, I ran out the door and hopped in the cab, pretending not to hear my mother calling me as we waited for a line of cars to pass before we could back out. After dropping off the books at the college library, we drove to the county dump and unloaded what remained.

The sun was beginning to set when we drove into our carport. My father walked out onto the front lawn and surveyed his work. There was an unmistakable look of pride on his face, the artist's satisfaction after creating order from chaos. He was not the only admirer. By this time there was a steady stream of cars going by our house, and I finally realized why. My mother realized too as she watched from behind the living room windows as the filled-up cars slowed to view my father's work. I went inside to find out my mother's reaction. She was shaking her head, obviously horrified at being the focus of the town's attention. "Oh Lord," she said. "I feel like I'm in a side show at the county fair." To make matters worse for her, Frank Moore had parked his car on the side of the road and was now aiming his camera at our home and grounds. My mother groaned, staggered over to a chair, and sat down.

In the next week almost everyone in Cliffside drove or walked by our home at least once. My mother, shy by nature, refused to leave the house, waiting behind closed curtains for the townspeople to tire of the spectacle.

As for my father, he went to bed that Monday night at 9:00 but was so sore the next day he could barely hobble to the bathroom, much less meet his class. My mother fed him breakfast and lunch in bed. His hands were so blistered he could not grip a fork. For the rest of the week, he moved with the stiffness and speed of a robot.

On Friday the *Cleveland County Messenger* ran a photograph of our house on the front page. The caption read: "The lovely home and well-maintained grounds of Professor James Hampton and his wife Linda." Nothing else was written, or needed to be.

I was never told the details, but my mother seemed to know my father's performance would never be repeated. Or perhaps it was not so much that he would not (with his obsessive nature, he might have devoted a good portion of his remaining years to making our yard his greatest work or art) as much as she herself had decided she did not want it repeated. Perhaps my mother had found out she could better bear embarrassment when it was spread out in small doses over the years. Or, finally, maybe my father's blistered hands and sore back were enough of a confirmation of his love to sustain her against the snide comments of the Mrs. Elys of the world.

As for me, I watched the grass quickly grow back. By late August, despite the dry weather, it was high enough to cover the metal "Yard of the Month" marker. I suppose that sometime in the last two decades I could have asked my mother how she and my father had come to an agreement about the yard. Was there an hour-long discussion, a few words, or was it just an unspoken understanding that the yard need never be maintained again, at least by her husband? But I never asked. I don't even know how my father became so proficient with a slingblade. How could he have learned such a skill growing up in a mill village? Had he once served time on a chain gang? After that late June day, anything seemed possible.

Raising the Dead

I t was the same week Dooley Ross drowned in Broad River that Mrs. Calhoun stood up in our church and announced she and Pappy, as she called her husband, were switching their membership from Cliffside First Baptist to Gospel Light Tabernacle Baptist, which is in the upper part of the county above Casar. Now neither event was really surprising. Dooley never could swim a lick, and as much time as he spent on the river it was only by the grace of God that he hadn't drowned sooner. As for Mrs. Calhoun and Pappy, Cliffside First Baptist was their third church in the last four years. They changed churches more often than most people change their oil filters. So far there hadn't been a congregation in the county that had dared not let her and Pappy join their church, and there wouldn't be one either, because Mrs. Calhoun owned the biggest cotton mill in Cleveland County. Almost every churchgoer in our county either worked at that mill or had relatives who did, so it wasn't surprising that every congregation made a big show of welcoming the Calhouns, no matter what people really felt.

Our church was no exception, though the deacons did hold a meeting about the matter of Pappy when Mrs.

Calhoun first let Preacher Thompson know they wanted to join our congregation. Since Pappy had been dead five years, it was one thing to allow him to be buried in the church cemetery, but it was another matter altogether to have a dead man become a voting member of your congregation. How could anybody even know if Pappy wanted to join our church? The deacons searched their Bibles and back issues of the *Biblical Recorder*, but there was nothing in writing either for or against corpses joining the church. Finally, they decided Pappy could join our church because Mrs. Calhoun believed it was what Pappy would have wanted, though the real reasons were that three of the deacons worked at Calhoun Mill and the other two were hoping Mrs. Calhoun would donate enough money to build a new softball field. As for Mrs. Calhoun voting for Pappy as well as herself on matters of church business, the deacons said it qualified as an absentee ballot.

So Pappy had been dug up like a flower blub and replanted under the oak tree in the oldest, nicest part of the cemetery. A good many people showed up to see the burial of a man many thought too spiteful to die. They stood in the shade of the oak tree and watched Jessie Hamrick and his men unload and then cover the most famous coffin in Cleveland County. And now, nine months later, here was Mrs. Calhoun standing up and telling us she and Pappy were leaving.

After Mrs. Calhoun sat down, young Preacher Thompson, who hadn't been out of seminary school much over a year, spoke a few words about how sorry he was Mrs. Calhoun was leaving the church and how he hoped she and Pappy would be happy at their new church and to please come back and visit with us anytime. He laid it on pretty thick, which I guess is a part of his job, but I expect he was like me and everybody else in the congregation, glad to have them on their way. But maybe Preacher Thompson was sincerely sorry. After all, it had been his idea to have the African missionary come to speak to us at Wednesday night prayer service the week before. Like I said, he was still wet behind the ears and didn't realize Reverend Aooka preaching in our church might upset anyone.

Actually, he was almost right. Almost everyone present enjoyed Reverend Aooka's message, especially the part about his early years as a cannibal before he found Jesus, but Mrs. Calhoun got up and left before Preacher Thompson had hardly finished introducing the Reverend, telling Ina Murrel, who was sitting beside her, that it wasn't right to have a negro, especially a foreign one who used to eat people, preach to civilized white folks.

And this was the reason, or so she said, that she was leaving our church, though a good many of us believed she just wanted a change of scenery, some different stained glass Bible scenes to look at on Sundays and Wednesday nights. Whatever the reason, they were definitely leaving, and you could almost hear the sighs of relief, especially from the members who worked at Calhoun Mill and had almost made themselves wall-eyed watching her out of the corners of their eyes, making sure they voted the same way she did every time we needed a show of hands on some church matter.

Like I said earlier, all of this happened the same week that Dooley Ross drowned. Dooley was as poor as the Calhouns were rich. While Mrs. Calhoun owned half the county, all Dooley had owned was his name and a couple of Zebco rods and reels. He had lived the last twenty years in a fall-out shelter out in Phil Moore's cow pasture. Phil had built it in the early sixties, believing that if the Russians fired a bunch of nuclear missles from Cuba, some of them were bound to be defective, like anything built by people who didn't believe in God, and would fall short of Washington and New York. Phil didn't charge Dooley any rent, though Dooley was expected to help mend the fences and bring back an occasional stray cow, but he did have to sign a paper in front of a notary public which said that in the event of a nuclear war Dooley would have to vacate the premises immediately, which I suppose was only fair considering Phil had been the one who built the shelter.

But Dooley probably wouldn't have been there anyway because he spent most of his time on the river fishing. He would bring what he caught back to town, selling some fish but mostly giving them away. He'd given me fish lots of times, and after Larry and me got divorced, Dooley helped me move furniture into my new house. It took a Saturday afternoon, but he wouldn't take any of my money.

The evening they found Dooley's body, Jessie Hamrick called me at home. Now a lot of people don't like undertakers just because of what they do for a living, but the way I see it an undertaker performs a needed service for a town. Jessie's an honest, decent man, even if he does wear his hair greased back like a t.v. preacher, but people are always making bad jokes about him, a lot of times to his face, or they try to avoid him as if death was catching. The one thing most people can't seem to do is accept him as he is. Maybe that is why I've always sort of identified with Jessie, because people, and not just men, treat me different, just because I'm a woman doing a "man's" job.

Anyway, Jessie was calling about Dooley, or at least his body. Dooley had no money, and though the county had a potter's field on the other side of Broad River, Jessie felt that Dooley deserved better than that, and I agreed. Jessie had already called around town and raised five-hundred dollars to buy Dooley a cemetery plot. Besides taking care of Dooley's body, Jessie was going to donate a headstone, and Phil Moore was going to buy him a suit. What Jessie wanted me to do was build Dooley a coffin. Jessie's cousin Bennie, who runs Hamrick's Lumberyard, had already agreed to supply the wood.

I felt it was the least I could do, so the next afternoon I quit work early and drove over to the lumberyard to get what I needed. When I got home I went out back and got two sawhorses out of the shed. I worked right through supper to get it finished, then called my Uncle Robert to come over and help me load it onto my truck. I called Jessie and told him I was bringing the coffin over to the funeral home.

Jessie had turned on the light to the back entrance so that was where I parked. He came out dressed in a pair of jeans and a flannel shirt, the first time I had ever seen him without a suit on. I knew it shouldn't bother me. Jessie had as much right to dress how he wanted to as anyone else, but it still bothered me a bit. It was like seeing your preacher in a bathing suit. We carried Dooley's coffin inside to a brightly-lit room with a tile floor and a stainless-steel table I was glad to see was unoccupied and laid it beside another coffin that had some wear and tear but still made the one I had built look like the blue-light special at K-Mart. Jessie took out a pack of Camels from his shirt-pocket and offered me one, and though I'd been trying to quit I took it. I thought it might calm my nerves. I wasn't used to passing my time with dead people.

"I reckon you know whose that one is," Jessie said, pointing with his cigarette to the other coffin. On the lid the word Calhoun was engraved on a piece of metal that had to be gold, meaning it was Pappy's, the most famous coffin in Cleveland County, maybe western North Carolina, rumored to have cost over five thousand dollars. People had come to see that coffin from as far away as Polk County when Pappy was buried the first time. Some people had even taken pictures when they carried it into the cemetery. Even now, that coffin could still draw a crowd whenever they were bringing it up or putting it back down.

Jessie looked at the coffin. "Nothing me or J.T. Blanton had over at his place was good enough for Mrs. Calhoun. She ordered it straight from Atlanta." Jessie took a draw on his cigarette. "See those handles. Sterling silver. And you ought to see inside it."

"I'd rather not if it's all the same to you," I said.

Jessie smiled for a moment when I said that, but his

eyes never left the coffin. "A lot of good folks' sweat paid for that casket," Jessie said. He wasn't smiling anymore, and I remembered that Jessie's momma and daddy had worked at Calhoun Mill.

"Where are you going to bury Dooley?" I asked, trying to change the subject, because Pappy's coffin had evidently brought back some bad memories.

"The only plot we can buy for five hundred dollars is over at Ebenezer Methodist Episcopal," Jessie said. "It would cost at least 750 dollars to bury him at a white church since he wasn't a member of any of them."

"Well," I said, "I don't think it's going to bother Dooley. Alive or dead he got along with black people as well as he did white folks."

"That's what I thought too," Jessie said. "So I called Reverend Conley, and he had a meeting with his deacons. Evidently there were some problems. Two deacons flat out said they didn't want their graveyard integrated. They claimed it was bad enough to have to live with white people, much less be dead with them. They also said it would hurt the property values of the surrounding plots, but the rest of the deacons said it would be O.K., provided I pay the five-hundred dollars up front."

"I suppose that's the best we can do for him," I said.

"I guess so," said Jessie. He pointed what was left of his cigarette at Pappy's coffin. "I reckon I'll take that old bastard's casket out to Gospel Light Tabernacle tomorrow morning. When I finish over there, I'll pick up Dooley's and carry it over to Ebenezer."

"Make sure you don't get them switched," I said. "Can you imagine Mrs. Calhoun if Pappy was accidentally buried in a black cemetery. She'd be fit to be tied."

Jessie and me laughed about that for a little while. Then he gave me a strange little smile, the same kind of smile a boy in the fifth grade makes when he's figured out a way to get a rubber snake into the teacher's pocketbook without getting caught.

"What if you just switched the bodies," Jessie said. "That way nobody would know."

"Poor Dooley," I said. "Pappy's coffin would probably be the nicest place he's ever slept."

"It could be done," Jessie said, "and none would be the wiser." Jessie was no longer laughing. He was serious as a heart attack.

"Listen," I said. "I better be going. It must be past nine."

"We could do it," Jesse said.

"I don't want to hear it," I said, moving toward the door. "There's no telling how many laws we'd be breaking."

"Three to be exact," Jesse said. He walked over to the corner where an ashtray was. "But no one would ever know. We could do it tonight. They ain't going to tell anybody," Jesse said, pointing at the two coffins.

I thought about the Calhouns and the kind of people they were, and I remembered how Pappy himself had fired my uncle twenty years ago for taking an extra ten minutes during a lunch break. But what finally persuaded me was thinking about how Dooley had never had anything when he was alive and how nice it would be if he could at least have something, a nice, silver-handled coffin and fresh flowers on his grave every week, now that he was dead.

"I hope you can get us a good lawyer," I said. "What do you want me to do?"

"I can do it all myself. That way you won't be involved," Jesse said, offering me another Camel, which I took. I figured I might as well, since smoking would be one of the few pleasures I'd be allowed in prison.

"I'm already involved," I said. "What do you want me to do?"

"You can help me put Dooley in Pappy's casket," Jesse said, and I immediately wished I hadn't volunteered. But it was too late now.

"Can you cover up his face?" I said. "I'd rather not see his face, especially after he's been in the river twenty-four hours. I'd rather remember what he looked like alive."

Jesse said that would be no problem, and if I wanted to, I could leave the room while he got what was left of Pappy and put it in the coffin I'd built.

A few minutes later Jesse called me back in, and we went into the next room where Dooley was stretched out on a stainless-steel table wearing the blue suit Phil had bought for him. Jesse had laid a towel over Dooley's face. When we finished putting him in the coffin, Jesse walked me out to my truck.

"It's not too late to change them back," he said. "Just tell me now if you don't want to do it. This time tomorrow will be too late."

"No," I said. "It's the right thing to do, even if it's wrong."

"Which funeral you going to tomorrow?" Jesse asked.

"Both," I said. "Provided I can make bail."

The next morning I drove up to Gospel Light Tabernacle and watched Jessie and his helpers plant Pappy's coffin in the ground again, though for how long no one but God and Mrs. Calhoun knew. She was there, of course, with all the supervisors from the mill and enough flowers around the grave to draw every hummingbird in the county.

Then I drove back to Cliffside and went to Dooley's funeral. The only people who showed up were me, Jessie and his men, Phil Moore and Reverend Conley. The reverend said a few words about how Peter and some of the other disciples had been fishermen and how Dooley was always willing to help another person out, either by giving them some of the fish he caught or doing some other favor. Then Phil put a plastic wreath next to the headstone, and we all went home.

All of this happened five years ago, and I'd like to think that the statute of limitations on those three laws has run out. In the last five years Dooley has been moved four more times, and Mrs. Calhoun has just about run out of Baptist churches . Rumor has it she and Pappy are planning to convert to Methodist. Jessie and me seldom speak about what we did, but each time Mrs. Calhoun calls him up and tells him it's time to move Pappy, he calls me, just so I'll know where Dooley is this month.

Between the States

Of course there's a good chance it's a bad idea, but that's exactly why I'm here. Ever since high school everything has been a bad idea, or at least turned out to be. Marrying Darlene, selling the farm, buying the monkey. I'm needing an industrial-strength dose of nostalgia. I'm thinking if maybe I'm around the people I went to high school with I might at least be able to remember again what it felt like when the future was something you could think about without wanting to crawl under a bed and howl.

I'm out in the parking lot behind the gym, the same parking lot where me and Darlene used to steam up the windows of my daddy's pick-up truck after basketball games, her in her cheerleading outfit and me in my basketball uniform, a hero, at least most games. That's the beautiful thing about high school. You might be a complete screw-up except for one thing—shooting a basketball well, shooting a bird in the FFA annual photograph, twirling a baton—and just doing that one thing well can make you a hero. But high school only lasts for awhile. That truck me and Darlene used to make out in, like everything else in my life now, ain't nothing but wreckage.

I take another swallow of the moonshine I bought from Junior Scruggs. It tastes like Prestone anti-freeze, but it's cheaper than anything store-bought. I made Junior put a match to the shine before I gave him the three dollars. It burned blue so I reckon I won't wake up blind.

Moonshine's making a comeback in the New South, and not just because it's cheap. So much is changing down here so fast people will buy anything that makes them feel like they're living in the South instead of some southern suburb of New Jersey. Southerners aren't worth a damn when it comes to change, and that's why God gave us moonshine and people like Junior to make it. I pour what's left into my hip flask and get out of the truck.

Inside the gym all of the lights have been turned off except for one on the stage. I'm standing near the doorway. There are a bunch of people in front of me, but it's too dark to make out who they are. "Stairway to Heaven" is playing on the loudspeaker system, the long version.

Robert Plant belts out a final wail and the song ends. The lights don't come on. Instead, Rodney Ruppe steps up to the microphone set up on the stage. I've known Rodney since the first grade, and he's always given me the creeps. When we were kids he was always catching toads and lizards and "operating" on them with a pocketknife and a pair of pliers. He's a doctor in Charlotte now, some kind of cancer specialist who owns two BMW's and a swimming pool that looks like a pair of lungs.

"I will now read the roll call of the dead," announces Rodney. He looks down at the paper and lets out a sigh, but you know he's thrilled, getting into this the same way he gets into looking for black blobs of disaster on X-Rays.

"Jimmy Battle. Cause of death, car wreck."

"Donna Beason. Cause of death, car wreck."

"T.J. Dawson. Cause of death, shotgun blast to the face."

Rodney looks down at the next name and smiles despite himself.

"Bobby Edmondson. Cause of death, liver cancer."

I try not to listen, but I can't help myself. Rodney reels off ten more names, and we aren't even to the M's yet. I need a drink bad, so I pull the flask out of my back pocket and swallow as much as I can get down without gagging. We finally get to Timmy Young, who hanged himself with 50 pound test fishing line.

"Let's have a minute of silence for our dear departed classmates," Rodney says. The auditorium light is switched off. Everything is dark and silent, and I can't shake the feeling that I'm dead too, that maybe when I fell through that glass door I went through another kind of door as well.

Then all the lights come on, and I know if I'm dead I must be in hell because Darlene is right beside me.

"What are you doing here?" she asks.

"Well, if you recall I graduated from this school too, the same year as you," I say.

"I know that. What I want to know is why you came?"

"Nostalgia, Darlene. The best years of our lives."

"Maybe your life but not mine," she says. "Not mine by a long shot." She turns to Stanley, who's eyeing me the same way he'd eye a dog someone brought into his clinic that was foaming at the mouth. Ever since I ran through the plate glass window after his fiancée, he thinks I'm dangerous crazy. He may be right.

"That's right, dear," he says, keeping his eyes on me. "I'm going to go get some punch Darlene."

"That's fine, honey," she says. "I'll join you in a sec. I just need to talk to Randy a moment."

Stanley puckers up his mouth like he's eating a lemon. "I'll miss you," he says as he pushes through the crowd toward the punch bowl.

"You could learn a lot about romance from that man," Darlene says. "We even have special names we call each other when we're," Darlene giggles, "intimate. He calls me Darling Darlene, and you know what I call him?"

"Possom Breath?"

Darlene ignores me, "Manly Stanley."

"Look, Darlene," I say, "I'm not really interested in you and Stanley's mating habits. If you've got something to say to me, say it."

"Yeh, I have something to say to you. You got the letter from my lawyer about when you have to be out of the house, right?"

"Yeh."

"Well make sure you are, because Stanley and I are moving in at 12:01 on the first, and we're going to have Sherriff Hawkins with us just in case you try to make trouble. And another thing," she says. "I know about you running that air-conditioner all day and all night. I talked to Carl Blowmeyer at Greene's Cafe last week. He says you got it set on 50 degrees. He also says you sleep on the floor now, naked except for a bunch of quilts wrapped around you. Blowmeyer's got proof too. He came over at 6:00 A.M. and filmed you and the thermostat through the window."

"So what's your point, Darlene?" I say.

"The point is don't try to stick Stanley and me with that last month's power bill when you move out. I've already alerted Duke Power."

"Anything else you want to say to me, Darlene, like thanks for the memories?" I try to sneer when I say it but it sounds more like a whine.

"Yes," she says, smiling. "Stanley had his sperm tested last week in Charlotte. He's got one of the highest sperm counts in the whole Southeast."

"Congratulations," I say. "Has he donated a sample to Ripley's *Believe It or Not* yet?"

Darlene sighs. "You need psychiatric help, Randy. Intense therapy, maybe for years. Stanley says you can't accept responsibility for your life, the mess you've made of it. Stanley says you're trying to retreat back into the womb when you wrap yourself up naked in those quilts."

"Look," I say. "You tell Stanley he needs to stick with analyzing his patients' brains, brains that are the same size as his own."

Darlene shakes her head. "There you go bad mouthing Stanley again when he's taking a professional interest in your case. Stanley's always interested in mental illness, whether it be animal or human."

"Is that why he's attracted to you?" I say.

Darlene glares at me, turns to walk away and turns back for the final word. "No," she says. "Stanley was attracted to me because of my love of animals and my sensitivity."

Sure, I think, watching her fine, long legs as she walks toward the punch bowl.

Up on the stage the band has set up after Randy's opening act. They call themselves Mutation and are fresh from a hot gig at the Amvets club in Shelby. They played at our senior prom twenty years ago and have lost a lot of hair since then but gained nothing in talent. The lead guitarist plays the opening chords of "Purple Haze" and then the singer joins in with about as much enthusiasm as a pithed frog.

I turn around to get the hell out of there, having gotten enough nostalgia for one evening, and almost run over Miss Prunty, my twelfth grade English teacher. She was ancient then, born at the turn of the century. She whips a wooden ruler out of a huge, black pocketbook and starts swatting me.

"Watch where you're going Randy Ledbetter," she screeches. "You're not too big to have to come over here next Saturday morning and clean the chalkboards. And just because Darlene's divorcing you is no reason to act like a hooligan either."

I try to get around her but she blocks the door.

"I'm not through with you yet, young man. I want you to tell me about this problem with your reproductive organs. Darlene told me a little but I want to know more."

I take the flask out of my back pocket and unscrew the cap.

"Hold out your hand, Miss Prunty," I say. "I just happen to have a sperm sample with me. You can examine it yourself."

The old bat staggers backwards, clutching her chest and moaning, but I know I haven't killed her. It'll take a stake through the heart to finish her off.

I dash through the doorway before she can recover. I take two steps before I knock the cigarette out of Phil Moore's mouth with my forehead. I'm thinking it would be easier to run a punt back against the Washington Redskins than get away from this place.

"Did you hear about Coach Beak?" Phil asks me, holding my arm so I can't get away.

"Who?" I say. Maybe it's the moonshine, maybe it's bumping heads with Phil, but the memory circuits in my brain are no longer working well.

"Coach Beak," says Phil," our old football coach. You remember how we used to say he wasn't human?"

I nod, the form of a flat-topped, bow-legged, tobacco-spewing bully becoming more and more clear in my memory, like one of those sixty-second Polaroid photographs.

"We may have been right," says Phil. "You remember Janice Hamrick?"

I nod, looking back over my shoulder to make sure Miss Prunty isn't coming after me.

"Well, she's been a nurse over in Shelby at the county hospital the last few years. She was working when they brought Coach Beak in last January for back surgery."

None of this is making any sense to me, but Phil has me by the shirt and he outweighs me by fifty pounds.

"Janice says she was prepping him for the operation when she saw it."

"Saw what?" I ask, and am almost instantly sorry.

"A tail," says Phil. "About six inches long, right at the crack of his butt. Had black fur all over it."

I jerk free from Phil and run toward the parking lot. I make it to the car and lean against the hood, gasping for breath.

"Do you remember me, Randy?"

Somebody's walking toward me out of the darkness, someone with long hair and wearing a dress.

"It's me, Randy, Lars. Remember?"

And I do remember. Lars had been an exchange student from one of those blonde-haired countries in Europe.

"Randy, you once told me you were disappointed when I first showed up in Cliffside, that you had hoped I would be one of those beautiful blonde women you'd seen in your father's *Playboy*."

Lars steps out of the shadows.

"Well Randy I am now. I'm not Lars anymore, I'm Laura."

I jerk open the pick-up's door, leap in, and lock the door.

"You Southerners are so provincial, says Laura as I roll up the inch of open glass between us.

I crank up the truck and spray gravel as I mash the accelerator to the floor. I don't dare look back. There's no telling what else from the past might be coming after me.

I don't know where I'm headed, just away, but I end up

at Broad River Bridge. I park the truck on the North Carolina side and get out. I walk onto the bridge, look down at the river. I think hard about jumping, thinking how they might never find me, the catfish and crawdads nibbling on me until I'd be nothing but a few bones washed on downstream miles from Cliffside, people all the while thinking I'd left for Charlotte or Atlanta.

But I know the'd find me, just like they found Dooley Ross when he drowned, and I know Darlene would tell people for the rest of her life it was about what she expected me to come to. I know, even if I was dead, that her doing that would bother me, that somehow the living can haunt the dead as much as the dead can haunt the living.

No, I'm not going to jump. That's the one thing in my life I am certain of.

It's almost dark, and you can see the lanterns of the fishermen flickering on up and down the riverbanks. The frogs and crickets are starting to talk to each other. I think about the river for a long time, about how it is between North Carolina and South Carolina, but not really in either one. I think about Miss Prunty, who is stuck somewhere in-between the past and the present. I think about Coach Beak and Lars, how they too are between two states. And that maybe I am too. What I'm thinking is that maybe I'm between the old good time of my life and the new good time of my life, and if I can just hold on for a while that the good time will come round again.

: Vincent :

Notes from Beyond the Pale

B ack when I was making that awkward transition from child to adult in the 1960s, it seemed Cliffside was the still point in a hurricane. Every morning the *Charlotte Observer* brought word of a world surging out of control. Every night at 6:30, I saw the race riots, the burning cities, the hippies out in San Francisco, the anti-war rallies, the war itself. But it was all black and white, in print and on the screen, and for that reason finally no more real to me then than the Hardy Boy mysteries I read or the adventure shows I watched on my family's decade-old Zenith.

This is not to say that the world outside Cliffside did not occasionally intrude. Eddie Hamrick was drafted in 1964, and Zak Murrel came home one Christmas from Chapel Hill with hair down to his shoulders and beads around his neck.

But Cliffside itself never seemed to change. Whenever I caught myself checking the cracks in the sidewalks to make sure they weren't getting any wider, that my world was about to shatter as well, all I had to do was walk into Benson's Drug Store. The candy bars were in the same place they had always been, in the same order—Butterfingers on the far left of the top shelf, then the Milky Ways, Baby Ruths, Mallo Cups, and Zero Bars. Milkshakes were forty cents, and if Mrs. Hendrix made it, she let you take the mixing cup to the booth. If Mr. Benson made it, he kept the extra for himself. Near the water fountain were dusty post cards with a picture of Cliffside Baptist Church on the front. As far as I knew, no one had ever bought one. They were just there, and I thought they always would be, like everything else in town.

Like Greene's Cafe, where the best deal, the special—a cheeseburger with lettuce and tomato, french fries, and sweet tea—wasn't even listed on the menu and cost between $1.25 and $1.50, depending on Marvin Greene's mood. Or McBee's Grocery where you could always buy a Coke a nickel cheaper than anywhere else in town. Or the Co-Ed Theater, where the popcorn was as bland and almost as old as the movies.

The handful who felt the town was stagnant and repressive moved to Charlotte or Atlanta. I'm old enough now to understand why some left. I'm also old enough to understand why most stayed: there was change enough in their individual lives—their waking up every day and seeing in the mirror they were older than they ever dreamed they could be. Unlike the children, the adults knew even Cliffside would change eventually, but they were content to let the town drag its heels, to hold out as long as possible.

And this is why during my fourteenth summer the return of Homer Caldwell from Massachusetts with a history degree and a new bride caused such controversy. By the time some members of the Cliffside Baptist Church's Women's Circle had come calling to welcome Homer's new bride and invite her to join their circle, they had already heard about Emily Caldwell's insistence on unsweetened tea at Greene's Cafe, even after Marvin Greene had explained he would have to make a special pitcher just for her. These women, one of whom was my mother, had also heard about her making Homer leave in the middle of the movie at the Co-Ed Theatre, hurting Marshall Hamrick's feelings, who, though he had not made the movie himself, had selected it as one he believed people in Cliffside would enjoy. When Mrs. Caldwell answered the door, she did not invite my mother or the other circle members inside. Instead, she spoke through the screen, telling Agnes Guffey, the group's spokeswoman, that she was agnostic. When Mrs. Guffey said that was O.K., she had been a Methodist before marrying Mr. Guffey, Emily Caldwell had locked the latch and said she was expecting a long-distance phone call. Then she had disappeared into the back of the house without saying another word.

Even that rebuff did not turn Cliffside against her. As my mother noted, Emily Caldwell had lived in the North all of her life and could no more help being rude than she could help talking like a clothespin had been clipped to her nose.

"She'll come around," my mother said.

Cliffside was so forgiving for another reason too. Homer Caldwell had always been a source of pride for the town. He had grown up on a chicken farm about a mile outside town, and though his family had never produced a high school graduate, Homer not only graduated from high school but had also been a National Merit Scholar, enabling him to attend Harvard on a full scholarship. Four years later the school board as well as the rest of the town had been delighted when he had applied for a teaching position at Cliffside High, because Homer was not just the smartest student in the school's history. People genuinely liked him. Despite his academic successes, he had never been conceited, had always been friendly, though quiet and shy, as if being so smart embarrassed him. Accepting Emily Caldwell was a way to ensure that Homer stayed.

It was a Thursday in August, two weeks before I would start the ninth grade, when Emily Caldwell's column appeared in the *Charlotte Observer* for the first time. As usual during breakfast at the Hampton household, we all had our noses in the newspaper as we ate. I was reading the sports, my father the used-car ads. My mother had disappeared behind the homemaker's section when she threw the paper onto the kitchen table as if it were on fire.

"That woman's done it now," my mother cried out. "Not even being a Yankee can excuse this."

"This was Emily Caldwell's first "Notes from Beyond the Pale" column, the subject of which was her visit from the Cliffside First Baptist Church's Women's Circle. My mother picked up the paper again, reading an especially offensive passage aloud:

> Only in a small Southern town such as Cliffside would strangers come to one's door to discuss one's most personal concerns. After they got through pitching their religious

views, I expected these women to quiz me on my political affiliation, how much we had paid for our house, and what brand of toilet paper I preferred.

"We were just trying to be neighborly," my mother tearfully told my father. "Can't she understand the difference between being friendly to a newcomer and being nosey?"

By noon everyone in town, whether they subscribed to the *Observer* or not, knew what Emily Caldwell had written in her column. Several people, including Agnes Guffey, wrote the *Observer* to complain but received only a form letter stating "the views expressed in the column are of an individual nature and do not necessarily reflect the views of the rest of the *Observer* staff."

In the next few months, Emily Caldwell's column addressed the problems of obtaining unsweetened tea in Greene's Cafe, the torn screen and lack of first-run features at the Co-Ed, and her account of shopping at McBee's Grocery where, according to her, the only seafood was Gordon's fishsticks. Worse, she wrote about her in-laws, making fun of their occupation in one column ("My in-laws spend more time with chickens than human beings") and their first names, Dewayne and Velma, in another. Even Homer was not spared. "Despite his Ivy League education," she had written, "my husband is starting to revert back. He is starting to drop his g's on word endings and to listen to hillbilly music. I suspect he will soon abandon his study of history to pitch horseshoes and shoot small mammals."

I had been in Homer Caldwell's history class for three months when this particular column appeared, and while Homer had indeed lost the last vestiges of a New England accent, I had no doubts about his ever losing his interest in history. The man was fanatical about the subject. In Mr. Caldwell's class everything that had ever happened was happening now. His lectures were always in the present tense.

His principal obsession was the Civil War. By November we had covered three and a half centuries of world history, bringing us to 1861. For two days Mr. Caldwell lectured on the prelude to the Civil War, concluding that perhaps at no time in history had better men fought for a worse cause. Mr. Caldwell then spent a full fifty-minute class period just on the attack at Fort Sumter, then three days on First Bull Run, mapping out troop positions in incredible detail, filling the blackboard, showing us where T.J. Jackson had stood like a stone wall, acquiring the nickname he would carry for the rest of his military career, where McDowell's troops had frantically retreated towards Washington. Mr. Caldwell never looked at a note or a book while he lectured. A movie reel seemed to be unwinding is his mind.

For a while it looked like the war might take longer to be taught than it had taken to be fought. At Christmas break we had only gotten to Shiloh. By the end of February we had fought with Forrest at Fallen Timbers, walked the plank road with Jackson at Chancellorsville, charged with Pickett at Gettysburg, and retreated with Joe Johnston to the outskirts of Atlanta. Finally, in mid-March, the war ended with Mr. Caldwell reciting Lee's farewell speech to his troops.

Not surprisingly, there were a few students in the class who found Mr. Caldwell's obsession with the Civil War comic. I would sometimes hear them before and after class laughing about General Caldwell, C.S.A. But for most of us his enthusiasm was contagious. As he spoke the final lines of Lee's last orders to his troops, Mr. Caldwell's eyes were not the only misty ones in the class. Laura Bryant actually broke into sobs, embarrassing everyone in the class, especially Laura, and causing me to make a feint in hopes of drawing attention away from her.

"Which general do you admire the most and why?" I asked Mr. Caldwell, expecting to hear about Lee, Jackson, of Forrest. Mr. Caldwell paused for a moment, looked out the window, westward in the direction of north Georgia and southern Tennessee.

"Joe Johnston,"he replied as the bell rang. "Because of his patience. He knew how to wait an enemy out, how to give an enemy enough rope to hang himself. Sherman would never have taken Atlanta if Johnston had not been replaced."

The Japanese still held Iwo Jima and the Germans Paris when the school year ended.

During the summer break, I saw Mr. Caldwell about as often as I had seen him during the school year. I was running five miles a day, getting in shape for cross country, and he was selling encyclopedias door to door. On my morning and afternoon runs I would see him dragging his satchel of samples around Cliffside, his white, long-sleeved dress shirt soaked with sweat.

Why Homer Caldwell was selling encyclopedias was the subject of considerable debate all summer. The majority opinion was Mrs. Caldwell was making him go door to door to support her extravagant tastes. The women in town had seen the dresses she wore only in catalogues before Mrs. Caldwell came to Cliffside, and Rusty McCoy, the town garbageman, gave regular reports of expensive dinners of lobster and wine, items acquired only by making a hundred-mile round-trip to Asheville. Since Emily Caldwell's only income came from her weekly column, surely money was needed to get through Homer's long, paycheckless summer. Others, however, believed it was a ploy to get away from Mrs. Caldwell, believing her such a monster that Homer found dehydration and possible heat stroke preferable to being cooped up in a house with her.

Whatever the reason, people invariably invited Homer in when he timidly knocked at their doors. They seldom bought encyclopedias, but they always brought him some lemonade or iced tea and listened to his sales pitch, keeping him out of the blazing sun and away from his wife at least for a little while.

Mr. Caldwell came to our house in July. My father was teaching summer school, but my mother and Betty Splawn were in the kitchen drinking coffee. I was with them, reading a book on Joe Johnston and drinking iced tea. My mother poured him a glass of tea, and we all sat down at the kitchen table. I showed Mr. Caldwell my Johnston biography. His eyes lit up for a moment, but then he remembered why he had come. He pulled his samples out of his satchel and started his fifteen-minute speech about the wonders of World Book. It was obvious he was as bored with what he was saying as we were hearing it. My mother said she'd talk to my father about buying a set, and Mr. Caldwell went wearily back out into the 95-degree heat, the satchel and its contents, which must have weighed twenty-five pounds, banging against his leg. Mrs. Splawn shuddered as she watched him limp across our yard toward Lula Hawkins' house.

"To think my nephew Wesley almost took that football scholarship to Syracuse before he changed his mind and went to Clemson," she said. Tears filled her eyes. "Wesley could have married one of those northern girls and ended up like that."

My mother placed her hand on mine and looked me in the eye.

"Promise me, son, that you'll never marry a Yankee," she said.

In the first week of August Emily Caldwell went North, without Homer. Cliffside's pessimists believed she had left to escape the fierce North Carolina summer for a few days, would return all too soon. The optimists took heart that Homer did not go with her, believed her gone for good. Once his wife departed, Homer stopped selling encyclopedias. Instead, he spent most of his time in Greene's Cafe, reading books on the Civil War as he drank glass after glass of iced tea, or he was at his parents' farm, helping out with the chickens.

Emily Caldwell returned the week school started back up. In her first column since her vacation Cliffside found out about a new addition, actually two, to the Caldwell household—a Rhode Island cock and hen Homer had brought back from his parents' farm:

> I had assumed that if my husband wanted a pet he would
> have gotten a dog or a cat, instead of a pair of chickens. He
> seems to be growing more and more nostalgic for the good
> old days back on the farm. I'm expecting him to build an
> outdoor toilet any day now.

"Now she's making fun of him because he wants to raise a couple of chickens," my mother said. "Lord knows he could use the companionship. Why on earth did that woman come back if it's so horrible down here, Earl? It's obvious she doesn't love Homer, and she hates everything about Cliffside."

My mother was speaking to my Uncle Earl, who had just finished bushhogging our back yard and was drinking iced tea with my mother and me before he headed back to his farm. My uncle contemplated the question for a few moments before giving his answer.

"There are people in this world who can be happy only if they are unhappy," my uncle said. "Unfortunately, these people never want to be happy in their unhappiness alone. So they marry people like Homer."

My uncle swallowed the rest of his tea, put on his John

Deere hat. "I've got to get back home. I've got an acre of hay to bail this afternoon."

Mr. Caldwell was not my teacher my sophomore year. I would occasionally see him in the hall between classes, but I read about him every week in the *Observer*. While Emily Caldwell's earlier columns had almost always been about matters outside of her immediate household, since her return from Massachusetts she had focused more and more on Homer and his chickens.

Homer was allowing some of the eggs to hatch as well as recruiting more adult roosters and hens from his parents' farm. Mrs. Caldwell published a running count of the Caldwell chicken population through the fall—twenty by Columbus Day, thirty by Halloween. Afternoons after school Homer could be heard hammering away in his backyard, building new coops for what his wife had dubbed Cliffside's first subdivision.

In her Thanksgiving Day column Emily Caldwell wrote she was no longer able to count the number of chickens, and it was no wonder, for what had once been a chicken subdivision now looked more like a chicken ghetto. Every square foot of the back and side yards was filled with chickens, often stacked two or three coops high. Homer had even built coops in the branches of trees. But there were always more chickens than coops. These ran free, congregating in the front yard as well as making occasional forays into the neighbors' yards. The smell of chicken manure was pervasive, the clucking, crowing, and chirping continuous. Ed Watt, who lived in the house closest to Homer, made a formal complaint to the town council. For the first time in Cliffside's history, there was talk of an ordinance banning farm animals within the city limits.

By this time it was obvious to anyone who read Emily Caldwell's column that "Notes from Beyond the Pale" had gone from being what the *Observer* radio ads called "a witty, open-eyed look at the foibles of small town life" to the ravings of a very disturbed person. Now Emily Caldwell wrote only about chickens. Homer was an afterthought. The tone of her column also had changed. When she told of leaving a car window down, then sitting on an egg when she slid behind the steering wheel, there was no hint of humor or sarcasm in her words, only horror.

"The chickens are getting to her," my Uncle Earl explained as we ate our Thanksgiving dinner. "Chickens, especially as many as Homer has, are never quiet. There will always be a couple of them clucking or crowing no matter if it's day or night. There ain't a moment that passes when that woman isn't aware she is surrounded by chickens. She may not know it, but she hears them in her dreams. It's like Vicksburg during the Civil War, except it's chickens, not Union soldiers."

My uncle paused, looked at my father. "What's the word that means you're always surrounded, always under attack?"

"Besieged?" my father answered, helping himself to some banana pudding.

My uncle smiled. "That's it. She is besieged."

Emily Caldwell's next and also last column seemed to confirm my uncle's view of Mrs. Caldwell's mindset, and it was a wonder the *Observer* ever ran it. The first line simply read "The sound of chickens," followed by a colon. "Cluck, cluck, chirp, chirp, crow" was all that was written on the next line, and each line after, all the way down to the end of the nine-inch column.

Two weeks later the *Observer* announced that Emily Caldwell's "Notes from Beyond the Pale" column had been discontinued because of "health reasons." She had also disappeared from Cliffside.

Many people assumed Mrs. Caldwell had gone north to spend the Christmas holidays with her family, but after January came and went and she had not returned, other theories arose. The most prevalent one was that she and Homer had gotten an divorce, but some, basing their opinions on Emily Caldwell's last column, believed she had been institutionalized. One or two people even ventured that Homer had killed her and buried her under one of the chicken coops. Clytemnestra Ely eventually asked Homer what had happened to his wife, but all Homer told her was that she "had gone away." That answer didn't satisfy Mrs. Ely, but it satisfied most of the town. Soon it was as if Emily Caldwell had never come to Cliffside at all.

III

Redfish, Possums, and the New South

I'm sitting in Greene's cafe drinking coffee and reading the want ads, just like I've been doing for the last few months, ever since Darlene quit me and I quit my supervisor's job at Hamrick Cotton Mill. There isn't much out there as far as job opportunities, especially for a guy who has made a solemn vow that he won't ever wear a necktie or dress shirt the rest of his life or even death, if they follow the instructions in his will. I'm looking for a job working on a farm, but there's nothing like that. All the blue-collar jobs are factory or construction. Nobody seems to be farming in the New South. Every time I turn around there's a mall where there used to be a cotton field, a factory where there'd been a pasture.

Gerald Crawly comes in and sits down on the stool beside me. He must smell my desperation, because the first thing he does is fold up my paper.

"You don't need to look at them want ads no more, buddy. I got a business deal gonna make us both rich."

Now six months ago I'd have just got up off my stool and told Gerald to take a hike, preferably to another state, but these are desperate times. I've been sleeping in the camper on the back of my pickup and bathing down at

Broad River. It's primitive, the way I am living. The way things are going, I'll be Cliffside's first street person, one of those guys that hasn't had his beard trimmed or hair cut in about four years, like the guys you hear about in New York City who go around grabbing their crotches and mumbling to themselves.

I've known Gerald long enough to know he is, as my granddaddy, a carpenter, used to say, half bubble off plumb. But like I said, things are getting tight, so I wave at Marvin Greene to bring me a refill.

"So how are we gonna get rich Gerald?" I say.

"Possum farm," he says, talking low, so no one else can hear him.

"What?" I say, already wishing I'd asked Marvin for my check instead of a refill.

"A possum farm, ranch, whatever you want to call it. A place to raise them."

"For what?" I say.

"To eat, of course," Gerald says.

I almost choke on my coffee. I put the cup down and wave at Marvin again. "Check," I tell him when I get his attention.

"Now just wait a minute," Gerald says. "You got to keep a open mind, like me."

"That's exactly your problem," I say. "Your mind is so open that peanut you call a brain has done fallen out."

"Well, you could at least listen to my idea." He points to my paper. "Don't look like you're exactly coming up with many brilliant ideas of your own."

Marvin brings the check but I don't get up because

Gerald's right. I haven't come up with anything on my own. It's already August, and that camper, and that river, are only gonna get colder come fall.

"Alright, Gerald," I say. "You got the time it takes me to drink this half cup of coffee to convince me."

"O.K.," he says. "First thing. You remember how during the depression a lot of people ate possum. My grandparents did, bet yours did too."

I nod. My grandparents had eaten possum, called them Hoover hogs.

"Yeah," I say, "but I never heard anybody talk about how good they were, and you may have noticed quick as people could find anything else to eat, they did."

"True," says Gerald, "but it proves one thing. It is physically possible to eat possum."

"So?" I say, taking a big gulp of coffee, trying to finish it off.

"Don't you see?" says Gerald. He's starting to get excited now. "All we got to do is start a trend. Then we got it licked."

"What kind of trend?" I say. "It's gonna take more than a trend to get people around here to eat possum. Too many people around here already know what a possum tastes like, or their parents or grandparents can tell them. Another thing, Gerald. People around here know what possums eat."

Gerald looks at me and smiles. "Who's talking about selling them around here. I'm talking about New York. Them people up there will eat *anything* if it's a trend. They'd eat baked cow shit if it were a trend."

Gerald reaches for his billfold. He takes out an article torn from a newspaper. He reads it aloud. "The two fish dishes most in demand this season are blackened redfish and catfish." Gerald stops and looks at the word for a few seconds and then gives up. "Catfish something." He starts reading again. "According to the chefs of the most famous restaurants in New York City."

Gerald hands me the clipping.

"Now I know you know what a catfish is, " Gerald says. "But you probably don't know what a redfish is, right?"

I nod.

"I do," he says. "When I was in the army I was stationed in Louisiana. Sometimes I'd go fishing with them cajuns. Everytime they'd catch one of them redfish they'd throw it back in the water or on the bank. Nobody ever took one home. They wouldn't let their cats eat them. A redfish ain't nothin but a cajun carp."

Gerald pauses, lets me think about that a minute.

"You go up to New York City today and order you a blackened redfish, you better get ten Abe Lincolns out of your billfold, cause that's what it's gonna cost you. I done researched it."

"Yeah," I say. "But a possum. They're so ugly. People ain't gonna eat something that ugly."

"Ugly," says Gerald. "You don't think a catfish is ugly? Or a mud turkle? They eat them too, you know."

"Yeah," I say, but at least a catfish doesn't have a long, pink tail, like a rat. People aren't gonna eat something with a rat's tail on it, Gerald."

"Well," says Gerald. "You might be right about that. But I've been studying on it. We can cut their tails off. Maybe if we keep cutting their tails off, we can breed it out of them."

I look at Gerald, his Cro-Magnon jaw and sloped forehead, and I'm thinking evolution is beyond Gerald in a number of ways, but the thing is, what he's saying, if you don't think about it too long, makes sense in a crazy sort of way.

"How much money we talking about, Gerald," I say, taking a sip of coffee.

"Two thousand dollars each," he says. "Profits divided sixty-forty my way, because it's my idea."

"What's the money for?" I ask.

"DeWayne Caldwell's chicken farm. He'll sell us his four chicken houses and the acre of land under them for four thousand."

"What about the possums, and feeding them?"

"That's the beauty of the thing," says Gerald. "Like you said, a possum will eat anything." He nods his head toward Marvin Greene. "I done talked to Marvin. We can get all the leftovers and tablescraps we want for free. All we got to do is haul them off."

"Yeah, but first we need some possums," I say.

"They're all over the place," Gerald says. "There ain't a day passes you don't see a possum around here. All we got to do is catch us a half dozen males, half dozen females. Boy, you think rabbits breed fast. You ain't seen nothing."

I take my last sip of coffee, get up to pay my bill.

"I'll have to think about it, Gerald. Think about it long and hard."

"Well," says Gerald, "don't think about it too long, because Larry Rudisell's already shown me two thousand dollars, cash money. But I'd rather do business with someone I can trust, which is why I'm giving you the first shot." Gerald pauses, looks over at the booth closest to us to make sure they're not listening. "But I can't wait too long. It's too good an idea for nobody else not to think of."

Larry Rudisell being interested gives me pause. Larry's crooked as a mountain road, but he's smart, businesswise. He's not gonna put his money into something unless he's pretty sure it's a good investment.

I turn around at the door. "I'll let you know something by tomorrow," I say.

I drive on down to Broad River, get my soap out of the camper and wade into the river. I'm buck naked when a bunch of teenagers come floating round the bend on innertubes. They're laughing and pointing at me as I scramble back up on the bank and hide behind some willow oaks. My life can't go on like this.

I've got an insurance policy I can cash in for twenty-five hundred dollars. I ain't got a wife. My daddy and momma are dead. My sperm is dead too, at least that's what the doctors told me and Darlene. So it's not like I've got anyone else to think about. Besides, another six months and I'll have spent it anyway on staying alive. As soon as I get dressed, I head for the bank in Shelby. Then I drive over to Gerald's house.

Gerald and DeWayne Caldwell sign the papers right after supper, and that night we're out on the blacktop cruising for possums. Gerald's right about there being plenty of possums around. The trouble is finding one alive. We count twenty-two, some that are probably still warm and some that are nothing more than a handful of hair and crushed bones.

It's past midnight when we crest a hill near Sandy Run Creek and see one alive, waddling down that white line in the middle of the road like a drunk failing a sobriety test. We're coming right at it but it doesn't even flinch, just stays right there in the middle of the road, like there's nothing in the world that it would enjoy more than having two thousand pounds of steel flatten it to the thickness of a Greene's Cafe pancake. I'm thinking there can't be anything stupider than a possum. Then I think about what time it is and what I'm doing and I reconsider.

Gerald swerves and slams on the brakes, pulls the car off on the shoulder of the road. He gets a burlap sack and a pair of leather gloves out of the backseat. The possum's still out in the middle of the road. We run up and hem it in between us, Gerald in front and me in the back.

"Grab him by the tail," Gerald shouts. "I'll hold the sack."

I bend down and the possum wheels around and hisses at me, bares a couple of yellow teeth that could do serious damage. I notice Gerald has put the gloves on.

"You pick up that son-of-a-bitch," I say. "I ain't letting that thing bite one of my fingers off. I'll hold the sack."

Gerald hands me the sack.

"Look," he says. "This is all you got to do."

He claps his hands together, hard. The possum flips over on its back. Its eyes are closed and its tongue is hanging out.

"That does make it easier, Gerald," I say. "But I'm still holding the sack."

The next morning I drive over to DeWayne Caldwell's place, our place now. Gerald's already there. He's hanging up a freshly painted sign that says "Possums for Sale: Wholesale or Retail." On the second line it says "The Cusine of the Rich and Famous."

"You left an 'i' out of *cuisine*," I say.

Gerald squints his eyes and looks at the sign.

"I can fix that later," he says. "Let me show you something."

Gerald takes me inside the chicken house closest to the road. Fresh straw covers the concrete floor. A pail of water is in one corner. The trough near the far wall is filled with scraps from Greene's Cafe. The possum is up on a beam about four feet above us, a band-aid wrapped around the nub where its tail used to be. The possum doesn't look like it's planning on coming down anytime soon.

"It's just going to take him a little time to get used to his new home," Gerald says. "Get a couple more possums in here and he'll be fine."

Gerald looks around. It's obvious he's pleased.

"I give him a name," he says, looking up at the possum. "The Opossum Paul."

"What?" I say.

"You know, like the disciple," he says.

Gerald knows as much about the Bible as he does evolution, but I don't even try to explain.

"The way I see it," Gerald says. "These possums are like the loaves of bread Jesus and his disciples fed the multitudes with. They just had a few at first, but then the bread kept multiplying, just like our possums are going to do."

"Does this mean you're going to name one Jesus too?" I say.

"I ain't sacrilegious," Gerald says, and walks off in a huff.

By the weekend we have Matthew, Mark, Luke, and Peter as well as Paul, but instead of the disciples it's more like that old singing group Peter, Paul, and Mary, because one of them has birthed a litter of eight.

In two months we have two chicken houses filled with possums. They're breeding like crazy, and I'm thinking if possums ever evolved into being smart enough to stay out of road they might take over the world.

By this time I've moved into the back chicken house, the smallest one. Fall's here and it's starting to get chilly at night. There's a portable heater in every henhouse, and while the possums have enough hair to stay warm I don't so I crank the heater up every night. There's a spigot with hot and cold running water, so I've even rigged me a shower of sorts. All of my stuff that was in the storage shed is here too. The chicken house is beginning to feel like home.

Although I'd been thinking about it for a while, it was Gerald who brought up my living out here. We'd been losing some of the smaller possums to weasels and black snakes, and Gerald was getting tired of driving out every night to make sure they were all O.K., so it made sense for me to be out here so that whenever there was a commotion I could chase off whatever was after them.

About this time I see Darlene for the first time in three months. Besides carrying off the scraps, I've been spending a few hours every afternoon at Greene's Cafe washing dishes, getting a free lunch and supper plus enough money to sustain me until me and Gerald strike it rich. She comes strutting in to pick up a takeout order. Darlene still looks fine with her long black hair and jeans so tight you'd think they'd been tattooed onto her.

She sees me looking at her from the kitchen and of course has to start bad-mouthing me.

"I've heard what you and Gerald Crawly are doing with those possums over at DeWayne Caldwell's old place, and I want you to know I think it's disgusting you're locking those poor creatures up and then cutting their tails off. I heard you all are trying to get people to start eating them." Darlene pauses to catch her breath and shake her head. "I didn't think even you would sink this low. Stanley's head of the Western North Carolina Veterinary Association, and he's already reported you and Gerald."

Stanley's her husband. He and Darlene are living in the home I worked ten years to help pay for, while I'm living in a chicken house.

"We're doing those possums a favor," I say, taking off my apron, ready to get out of here. "Gerald and me are getting them off the roads, protecting them. They'll live a lot longer inside our possum hotels than they will outside.

They'll eat better too. And after they've lived a long and happy life, we may kill them, but at least their death will have more benefit than being squashed out on some two-lane."

Darlene gives me a look as withering as the July sun.

"Besides," I say. "Since when have you become so enamored with possums? Every time one got in our garbage, you wanted me to go out there and blast it to bits with my shotgun."

"Stanley's enlightened me," she says.

"Yeah, right," I say. "You tell Stanley he's killed more animals on his operating table than Gerald and me will kill if we stay in business a hundred years."

I throw the apron on the counter and walk out the back door of the cafe before she can reply. I'm not married to Darlene anymore so I don't have to talk or listen to her. The constitution protects me from cruel and unusual punishment.

By late November we have all three chicken houses filled to the max. It's clear we've got to start selling or start letting some go.

"Alright," says Gerald on Thanksgiving eve. "The hard part's over. Now all we got to do is start the trend."

"How we gonna do that?" I ask, already knowing whatever he's about to say is going to be as harebrained as the rest of this scheme.

"Don't you worry about that," says Gerald. "By the way, I want you to eat Thanksgiving lunch with me tomorrow."

"At your mother's?" I say. I haven't had turkey and dressing in a year, or much of anything homecooked, so I'm hoping hard.

"Naw," says Gerald, "at Greene's Cafe."

"But he's closed tomorrow."

"Not for us," says Gerald. "You just be there at twelve tomorrow and bring an appetite. I'm buying."

Gerald takes his leather gloves out of his back pocket. "By the way, I'm going to take Paul with me tonight. He's been here the longest and could use a change of scenery. I'm gonna let him run loose in my basement, have some time to himself."

The next day right at noon I walk into Greene's Cafe. Gerald is already there and so is Frank Moore from *The Cleveland County Messenger.*

Gerald walks over and slaps me on the back.

"Hungry?" he asks, wearing a smile a little too wide to make me comfortable.

"For sure," I say. "I didn't eat any breakfast, just a glass of orange juice."

"Good, good," says Gerald. "Just have a seat at our booth. Lunch is on its way."

"What's Frank Moore doing here?"

"Reporting," Gerald says a little too fast. "Just go have you a seat."

Marvin Greene is back at the grill. I can't see what he's cooking but I sure as hell can smell it, and it ain't turkey. I'm not even sure it's edible. Marvin's shaking salt, pepper, oregano, Texas Pete, and anything else he can find on the shelf above him onto what he's cooking, but it's not doing any good as far as I can tell. Then I realize.

"Oh, no," I say, getting up. "You can forget it, Gerald."

I'm halfway out the door before he catches me. Gerald pulls me back inside, talking fast and soft because Frank Moore is looking our way.

"You got to ," he whispers. "Somebody's got to go first, partner, and it's got to be us."

"No way, Jose." I turn back to the door.

"This is it," he says. "I called up Frank Moore so he'd write it up. We back down now and we'll never sell a possum. Frank will make a laughingstock out of both of us."

Gerald looks me in the eyes. "But if we eat it, it's the beginning of a trend. This is just how that redfish craze started, one dinky restaurant down in New Orleans started serving it. One newspaper article later they were on their way. Next stop the Big Apple."

I look back into Gerald's eyes, and I know he is completely crazy, a lunatic, but I also know that only a lunatic would have listened to him in the first place. But it's too late to turn back now. Crazy or not, Gerald and his plan are my last best hope.

"Besides," says Gerald, "I done paid Marvin twenty-five dollars to open up and cook it for us, and that don't even include the new skillet I have to buy him when he gets through."

"O.K. Gerald," I say. "O.K."

Marvin brings us our tea and silverware. Then he brings

our plates which have a roll, sweet potato, and grey piece of meat Gerald is calling possum steak.

"Do you want to bless it?" Gerald says, "or me?"

"I think both of us better," I say.

Frank Moore comes over to our booth with his camera.

"Bon appetit," Frank says as Gerald and I lift a forkful of the grey meat, put it in our mouths, and slowly start chewing.

Monday afternoon Gerald's car screeches to a stop outside the possum hotel closest to the road. I'm inside pouring fresh water in the pails when Gerald rushes in and thrusts a newspaper in my face.

"That man calls himself a journalist?" screams Gerald, his face red as a beet. "Just look at this."

On the front page is a picture of Gerald and me looking a little grim and peaked. Underneath the picture the headline reads "Local Men Eat Possum, And Live."

"You call that objectivity?" Gerald says. He snatches the paper from me and begins reading. "The smell of rancid flesh per, per. . ."

"Permeated," I say.

"Permeated Greene's Cafe Thanksgiving day."

Gerald looks at me. "Rancid. How does he know it's rancid? He wouldn't even taste it."

Gerald throws the paper down, stomps on it while possums scramble into the corners.

"He's ruined us," Gerald moans. "That four-eyed son-of-a-bitch has done gone and ruined us."

Gerald kind of half kneels, half collapses onto the floor.

"I spent all morning calling restaurants in New York, just begging them to try our possums. I offered them free of charge. I even offered to pay the shipping. They hung up on me, every one of them."

Gerald stops talking. A car has pulled up outside. A man in a dark business suit gets out.

"Oh no," whines Gerald, assuming a fetal position. "This can't be nothing but more trouble."

The man comes inside, doesn't even look surprised that Gerald is wallowing around like a rabid animal. As a matter of fact he acts like it's about what he expected.

"I assume you two gentlemen are the owners of this establishment," he says.

We nod.

"My name is Pinkney Boatwright, and I am from the Western North Carolina Alliance to Prevent the Imprisonment of Wild Animals."

"Now look here," says Gerald, getting up off the concrete floor. "We got all the required licenses. You go check at the courthouse in Shelby if you don't believe me."

"At the request of Dr. Stanley Burns, I have checked," says Pinkney Boatwright. "Unfortunately, you are correct."

"So why are you here?" says Gerald, starting to bristle up. "What business you got with us?"

"We, my organization, want to make a deal with you," Pinkney Boatwright says as a possum comes over and sniffs his shoe, decides it's not edible and moves on. "We don't believe this opossum cuisine fad you're trying to start will catch on, but we don't feel we can take a chance."

Pinkney Boatwright clears his throat, starts talking to us

like he's giving a lecture. "As I'm sure you are not aware, the sudden popularity of the redfish led to overharvesting and an ecological nightmare in Louisiana. If the opossum were suddenly to be overharvested as the redfish was, the ecological balance could be seriously disturbed."

"So?" says Gerald.

"So," says Pinkney Boatwright. "Dr. Burns and his wife assured me that appealing to you to release the opossums as a matter of propriety and conscience would be useless, so our organization is willing to offer you eight thousand dollars if you will release the opossums and sign a statement that you will not raise opossums or any other undomesticated animals."

"Eight thousand dollars," Gerald shouts. "Man, that doesn't even begin to cover our costs, the blood and sweat we've poured into this business. The chicken houses and land are worth that alone."

"I've researched the deed," Pinkney Boatwright says. "You paid four thousand dollars for the land and these chicken houses. Eight thousand dollars is extremely fair, especially considering we do not want either the chicken houses or the land. We will also coordinate the release of the opossums so that they do not overpopulate one region of the county."

"Fair," screams Gerald. "It's twelve thousand dollars or nothing."

"I suppose then there is no need to further pursue this matter," says Pinkney Boatwright.

I grab Gerald and push him outside, out of hearing range.

"Listen," I say. "If you don't tell that man we're taking

his deal, I'm going to kill you and feed you to the possums." I shake him hard. "You understand, Gerald?"

Gerald nods.

"O.K.," I say. "Let's get in there and take that man's money before he realizes what a mistake he's making."

I take my forty percent share and buy out Gerald's part of the farm, buy me some chickens from DeWayne Caldwell's son, and refurbish my chicken house, make it into a real home, with a kitchen and a bathroom and even a screened-in porch. It's April now and I'm selling enough eggs that I no longer have to wash dishes at Greene's Cafe. Every evening after I check on the chickens, I put a Patsy Cline album on the stereo and a beer in my hand. Then I sit on the front porch as me and the chickens start to settle down for the night.

Judgment Day

After a few weeks had passed and the Methodists and a number of Baptists from other congregations had tired of asking, "You still among us" to anybody who had been there that Sunday, and after everyone in Cliffside had finally figured out exactly *what* had happened, there was still some questions about why it happened.

People outside the church said about what you would expect them to say, that it was a combination of coincidence and overactive imaginations. A few in the congregation, including my ex-husband, Larry, who would know if anyone would, claimed it was the devil's work. But for most of us who had been there that Sunday, it was hard not to see it as a true act of God.

It was one thing to have Sandy Run creek flood the church cemetery. After all, sixteen inches of rain had fallen in twenty-four hours, the most ever on record in the county. By late Sunday morning it was hard to find anything that wasn't under some water. And it was within the realm of coincidence that on the very Sunday rain flooded the whole county, Preacher Thompson might preach on the apocalypse.

But how could you explain Rudy Holland's sudden craving for waffles after eating fried chicken every Sunday for almost half a century? That was what stumped people, flat out baffled them. It had to rain a record-setting amount sometime. Records are made to be broken. Preacher Thompson eventually had to preach a sermon on the second coming. Some preachers I've heard preach on little else. But like I said, there was no earthly way to explain Rudy's sudden craving for a Sunday lunch of waffles. According to Lola, his wife, Rudy didn't even like waffles much, even for breakfast.

Rudy couldn't explain it either. When people around town asked, all Rudy could do was shrug his shoulders and tell whoever asked that it was an impulsive thing, like when he decided to take harmonica lessons. He also couldn't explain why he bought the syrup before church instead of after. Or why he went to Washburn's Quik-Stop instead of Buddy Brown's store, which only carries Log Cabin. Or why last January he had rigged up his truck horn to play "Heartbreak Hotel" whenever he pressed the steering wheel.

Which was not to say Rudy couldn't explain some things, like why he'd had a wreck that Sunday. According to Rudy, by the time he and Lola had finally decided on Mrs. Butterworth's instead of Log Cabin or Dixie Darling, they were already five minutes late for church, so it wasn't too surprising Rudy might take the curve at Phil Moore's farm a little fast, especially for a rainy day, and run off the road and into Phil's cow pasture, not able to stop till he and Lola crashed into a hog pen that was, fortunately, empty.

What else was there to do to get help but blow the horn when they couldn't get either door open? How could Rudy or Lola know what "Heartbreak Hotel" would sound like a quarter of a mile away at the church, during a thunderstorm?

But like I said, to really understand you had to be there in the church that Sunday, and I was, sitting on the third row between Uncle Robert and Harry Bayne. Only about a quarter of the congregation was there. Several bridges had been washed out during the night, and it was still pouring down rain and thundering. To get out in such weather was hard, even dangerous, and you could hardly blame anyone, especially anyone with kids, for just staying home. Which probably made some people's day, there being nothing better for some folks than an excuse not to go to church. They surely had one this Sunday and took full advantage of it.

But the people you'd expect to be at the eleven o'clock service were: Phil Moore and his wife and kids. Jack and Anna Benson. The widows: Ina Murrel, Lula Hawkins, and Janet Blanton, who always sat together on the front row. Miss Annie Scruggs, who had forty-two years of perfect attendance and would have water skied to church if it meant keeping her streak intact. And Ed Watt, sitting near the back by himself, like he always did. My ex-husband Larry was there too, with his fiancée Wanda Wilson, though he has no more interest in religion than a mud turtle. Like he'd told me years back, as a car salesman he was a pillar of the community, though "pillow" of the community was more like it, considering how many beds he'd tried to get into over the years.

A couple of minutes after 11:00, when it was clear no one else was coming, Preacher Thompson said a brief prayer, then told us to open our hymnals to number 333, "When the Roll is Called up Yonder." With the rain pounding the roof and a crack of thunder every thirty seconds or so, you could hardly hear the singing or the organ, which was a merciful thing since none of the choir members were present and Anna Benson, who was subbing on the organ, was showing why she'd lost her starting job to Cindy Putnam two years ago.

We got through all four verses, as well as the congregational prayer that followed, but Preacher Thompson decided to have pity on us all and cut out the other two hymns we were scheduled to sing before the sermon. So after the announcements and the Old Testament reading, Preacher Thompson dove right into his sermon, reading from chapter 20 of Revelations, almost shouting to be heard over the storm. The electricity had been out since the opening prayer, and the church was dark and shadowy, making Preacher Thompson's reading aloud the verses about the earth and sea giving up the dead even spookier.

Then Preacher Thompson actually started into his sermon. "Many have wondered if it will be our generation that witnesses these events," Preacher Thompson said "Billy Graham has noted..." But we never found out Billy Graham's opinion, because at that moment a gust of wind blew open the doors at the back of the church. Jack Benson got up to close the doors, but he closed only one before he pointed a finger toward the cemetery, letting the rain drench his suit while his mouth opened and closed like a fish on a riverbank. "Preacher Thompson," Jack finally croaked. "You better come here."

Preacher Thompson let his sermon notes drop to the floor and ran down the aisle, but by the time he got to the back of the church he had to get in line to see what Jack was pointing at.

Out in the flooded graveyard three coffins floated like johnboats among the half-submerged tombstones. It was too much for Lulu Hawkins, whose husband was buried out there. "It's Judgement Day," Lulu screamed, then fell backwards into Ed Watt's arms. By that time it was hard not to believe Lulu was right, because not only had the dead risen, but now we could hear Rudy Holland's horn blasting across Sandy Run Creek, and while it may not have sounded exactly the way we might have thought Gabriel's trumpet was supposed to sound, what did we have to compare it with?

Everyone looked at Preacher Thompson, figuring if anybody knew what to do it would be him. But evidently seminary school had failed to provide a plan of action for this day, which, in my opinion, was a pretty serious oversight, kind of like a quarterback being sent into the Super Bowl without any idea of what plays to run.

Preacher Thompson winged it as best he could, telling us that he felt the best thing to do under the circumstances was simply to continue the service. So he picked up his notes, waited a few moments for Lulu, who was lying across one of the pews, to quit moaning, and began again.

But quick as Preacher Thompson could say Billy Graham, Phil Moore stood up and raised his hand to get Preacher Thompson's attention. "There's something I want to get off my chest," he said. Then Phil turned and faced all of us. "The last eight years I've been going down to Gaffney to drink a couple of beers on Friday afternoons. Now I don't get drunk, and I don't play the poker machines, but it still ain't right." Phil turned and faced Preacher Thompson again. "Sorry to interrupt you, Reverend, but I just had to get that off my chest."

Phil sat down, looking embarrassed and relieved at the same time. His wife gave him a hug. Of course, just about everyone in the congregation already knew Phil spent some time at Harley's Lounge on Friday afternoons. Gaffney is only twelve miles from Cliffside, and plenty of people had seen Phil's truck parked outside.

Preacher Thompson tried to start again, but he hadn't got a sentence out when Janet Blanton raised her hand. She turned around and looked at Ed Watt near the back of the church. Ed looked like he was trying to decide whether to run out the door or crawl under a pew. "I just want to say that Ed and me have been seeing each other the last three years," Janet said. Lulu Hawkins almost fainted again when Janet said that. She'd known Janet since they were kids, but like the rest of us she hadn't a clue. Unlike Phil's confession, this confession was news. "I haven't been going to visit my aunt in Charlotte when I go there," Janet said. "I've been meeting Ed at the Days Inn downtown."

Janet turned a shade redder when she realized what she'd said. "What I mean is, we both stayed in the same motel but in separate rooms." Then Janet's voice got a little quieter. But we do go out to some of the night spots, and sometimes I'll drink me a pina colada." Janet took a deep breath. "And sometimes we dance."

After Janet finished, you would have thought confessing sins was Cleveland County's new favorite sport. Everybody seemed to have their hands up, and Preacher Thompson was nodding at one hand and then another, like an auctioneer trying to take bids. Ina Murrel confessed she'd had impure thoughts about the WSOC weatherman. Uncle Robert stood up and admitted he had never paid income tax on the money he'd made selling cantaloupes out of his garden. Miss Annie admitted that she'd missed church on January 12, 1957, and Phil Moore's little daughter, Cora, confessed she'd glued their cat Tammy's tail to the floor while it was asleep. Harry stood up, too, confessing he kept a box of *Playboy* magazines in his basement.

I was less than thrilled to hear I was competing with Miss October, but when Harry sat back down I didn't say anything. Instead, I stood up and had my say, telling Preacher Thompson and the rest of the congregation that I hadn't always behaved like a Christian should, that I had been hard hearted and unforgiving towards Larry and had actually been glad when he'd had his accident last March.

Larry, of course, was not to be outdone, so as soon as I sat down he jumped up and admitted he had been unfaithful when he had been married to me, which of course everyone already knew, and that he had spread false rumors about me as well.

That would have been enough confessing for anyone else. But at that moment an especially loud clap of thunder shook the church. Larry turned a little paler and looked up at the roof like it might collapse on all of us any second. "I have also put sawdust in gear boxes and rolled back odometers," he quickly added.

Wanda wasn't a member of our church, but that didn't keep her from standing up when Larry finished and admitting that she'd lied to Larry when she told him she had been at a Tupperware party last Thursday night. Instead, she had been in the back seat of Billy Ledford's Buick. Larry looked like he was ready to strangle Wanda but seemed to think better of it when thunder shook the church again, followed by a knock on the back door.

Lulu Hawkins, who up to this time had been too dazed to confess, held onto the arm of the pew and turned toward the door. "Harold, if that's you," she said, "I know I was wrong to just let you touch me on major holidays. I know you had needs as a man. Forgive me," Lulu said, fainting again.

The doors swung open and Sheriff Hampton, his deputy Tommy Clark, and Jessie Hamrick came in, their hats in their hands. "Sorry to interrupt your service, Preacher," Sheriff Hampton said, "but the creek's flooded the graveyard. Some of the coffins in fresh graves have come out of the ground." The sheriff nodded his head toward Jessie. "Jessie feels like we should put them in the church until the water goes back down. It's about quit raining, so in a minute or two we might start bringing them in, if you all have no objection."

Preacher Thompson said we were just finishing up, so he said a quick prayer and then we all followed the sheriff out of the church. Outside it was still drizzling, and you could still see a flash of lightning back towards town, but the sun was breaking through the clouds for the first time in a day and a half. Over at the edge of the cemetery, Jessie Hamrick was explaining to Preacher Thompson and most of the rest of us what had happened to the coffins, telling how they buried people above ground in New Orleans because there the graveyards flooded every time it rained.

Harry and I were standing beside Phil Moore, and after Jessie finished his explanation Sheriff Hampton walked over to tell Phil about Rudy driving into his hog pen. "We got him and Lola out on the way over here," he told Phil.

Like I said, most everyone was at the edge of the graveyard, except Larry, Wanda, and Jack Benson, who had bought a car from Larry a few weeks back. They were in the parking lot, raising a ruckus. Larry was yelling at Wanda, saying he was calling off the engagement and to give him his ring back, which she did, but not before telling Larry what a sorry s.o.b. he was. Jack Benson was seconding what Wanda was saying and threatening Larry with a lawsuit to boot. At least for Larry, it truly was judgment day. He finally make a break for it, jumping in his Pontiac and swerving out of the parking lot.

As for the rest of us, the scene in the parking lot reminded us of what we had said in the church, but as I looked around at everybody else, I could tell they seemed to feel like me, a little embarrassed but feeling pretty good all in all, like the rain had not only washed away a couple of bridges but also a lot of dirt and trash that had been accumulating in our hearts for too long a time.

Finally, people started to leave, including Ed and Janet, who were holding hands as Ed walked her to her car. Harry told me he'd be over to eat Sunday lunch with me and Uncle Robert, but first he wanted to take some trash he'd been keeping in his basement to the dump. I got in my truck and cranked it up. Up the road, Wanda was walking towards town, her high heels turning an ankle about every fifth step. I stopped and gave her a ride. I never much liked her, but it seemed the Christian thing to do.

: Vincent :

My Father's Cadillacs

I was 15 when I came home from track practice one late April afternoon to find a big, light-gray car under the blooming dogwood tree where our blue Plymouth was usually parked. That the car might be ours didn't occur to me, because everybody I'd ever seen who owned this kind of car had money and a big white house to go along with it. No one in my family ever had either.

Our cars had been battered Plymouths and Mercurys which came with six-digit mileage figures and engines that broke down on long trips. The seat covers were ripped, the tires were bald, and the heaters seldom worked. But I had never been ashamed of our cars because most of the people around Cliffside owned similar ones. Doctor Wasson was the exception, and he was the man I thought of when I hurried into the house, expecting to find my mother or father sick or injured. I didn't even remember that his car was light green. Inside, however, I found only my mother and father.

The car belonged to my family.

"It's a Cadillac, isn't it," I asked, "like Doctor Wasson's?" My father proudly answered that indeed it was. My mother said nothing. It was clear that she was not nearly as happy about our new car as my father was. I ran back outside.

It was a Cadillac, but hardly the equal of Doctor Wasson's. This one was almost 10 years old, and though it had electric windows like Doctor Wasson's, only two of ours worked. Ours had a cigarette lighter, clock, and an AM/FM radio; none of these accessories worked either. Nevertheless, being used to the Plymouths and Mercurys, I was impressed with the fact that these gadgets had ever worked.

My enthusiasm for our new car was short-lived, however. Within three days, Jimbo Miller, who sat behind me in homeroom, poked the back of my head with a pencil.

"Why did your old man buy that bone car?" Jimbo asked.

"What are you talking about, Jimbo?" I said, knowing I really didn't want to know.

"That Cadillac," he hissed, because Miss Blanton was looking our way. "Everybody in town is talking about it. That car could only come from one place. I know. When my uncle died last year, I rode in a car just like it."

"Doctor Wasson has a Cadillac," I said.

"Yeah, but his is green, and he bought his brand-new, not from a funeral home. Besides, he's a doctor. I think there's some law that they have to drive Cadillacs."

I was too stunned to speak. At the handful of funerals I had attended, undertakers had always terrified me. Dressed in their black suits, they always seemed to be tall, thin, pale men whose smiles were as phony and awful as the smiles on my dead relatives' faces. Once a funeral director had shaken my hand, and his soft, clammy hand had made me shudder.

"Face it, boy," Jimbo said. "Your old man has done lost his mind and bought an undertaker's car, and you're going to have to ride in it. Hey, there might even be a body or two in the trunk."

Jimbo snickered, stopping only to repeatedly whisper "bone car" into my ear until I finally turned around and punched him in the nose. Bleeding from both nostrils, Jimbo finally shut up, at least for a little while, but I had to stay after school a week for hitting him, and Jimbo made it absolutely clear to all my classmates exactly what kind of car my family now owned.

In the next few days I wondered why my father hadn't just made me wear a sign around my neck with "not normal" written on it, instead of buying a 1960 Cadillac. I suffered the cruelest blow when Laura Bryan, a girl I had been secretly in love with since the sixth grade, asked me if my family's new car really had once been owned by a funeral home. I survived fifth and sixth periods only because it was Friday, and I knew that as soon as I stayed my extra 30 minutes after school for hitting Jimbo, I could skip track practice, walk home, lock myself in my bedroom, and never come out for the rest of my life.

I did, of course. The smell of pork chops brought me out. But while eating supper I told my parents that our new car had wrecked my life. My mother said nothing, though she was obviously less than thrilled about the Cadillac herself. My father was staring out the window at the dogwood tree, deep in thought about something else. This made it worse. He wasn't even listening to what I was saying. As soon as I finished my banana pudding, I went to my room, locked the door, and brooded the rest of the evening over the tragic turn my life had taken. I came out the next morning, but only after I heard the roar of the Cadillac's 450 engine, signalling that my father was on his way to the art department where he spent most Saturday mornings and afternoons painting and throwing pots.

I found my mother in the kitchen drinking coffee and reading the newspaper, used to these husbandless Saturdays. Why, I asked her, had my father picked, of all the thousands of used cars in western North Carolina, the one that would make my life miserable? But she had no idea why. He had just driven the Plymouth up to Asheville one morning, and in the afternoon he had come back with the Cadillac.

"Your father doesn't always have a reason for the things he does. You surely know that by now," she said.

I did know. I understood exactly what my mother meant. This was the man who had taught classes in his bedroom slippers, forgetting to put his shoes on before he left home, who on trips kept my mother and I constantly on the alert, knowing from experience that my father might drive right by our destination.

And there were other things, caused not so much by forgetfulness as by just not knowing how normal human beings were supposed to act. Several times late at night I had gotten up to get a drink of water, turned on the kitchen light, and found my father in his underwear leaning against the kitchen sink and staring out the window at the moon as he ate a banana. Or we would go visit my mother's family and my father, after barely saying hello, would sit down in the nearest chair and read a book about Italian painting until it was time to leave.

Nevertheless, I was convinced there was something different about my father's recent behavior. For one thing, buying a car was something you had to know you were doing. No one, not even my father, could go out and buy a car without realizing it. I knew my parents had recently paid off the final installment of my father's student loans, but we were still far from being well off. His income was no better than most of the mill workers or farmers around Cliffside. Our new car clearly made this point. It was a Cadillac in name only, and my father could have gotten a nicer, newer Plymouth or Mercury for less money and less trouble. Cadillacs, even used ones, were rare in rural North Carolina.

So why a beat-up old Cadillac? I'd always believed that in his own quiet way he loved me. When I was younger he had always been the one who woke me from my nightmares and stayed with me, sitting on the corner of the bed until I fell asleep. He had even shared my intense though short-lived interest in snakes. Had this man secretly hated me all the while, and was he only now allowing himself to show it by buying a car that would make me an outcast among my peers?

"You know," my mother said, trying to cheer me up, "it could be worse."

"I doubt it," I said.

"He wanted to name you when you were born, and the name he picked out for you was Hieronymus Michelangelo

Hampton. I told him no child of mine was going to go through life with a name like that."

My mother was right. With a name like Hieronymus I wouldn't have survived past the first grade, much less adolescence, at least not in Cliffside, North Carolina.

"You see, it could have been worse," she said.

Despite my vow never to leave my room again, I was in school on Monday morning. I sulked down the hallways between classes, expecting the worst. But except for a few remarks, I found my family's Cadillac no longer a hot topic of conversation. Evidently, our car had been talked about around town for a few days and then dismissed by the adults as just another example—like Professor Hamrick's unzipped pants and Professor Abrams' refusal to get a driver's license—of the bizarre behavior of the college's teachers, behavior they forgave because they had come to view it as an inevitable affliction of the overeducated. Their children followed suit.

Still, I was already beginning to dread the day, now ten months off, when I would turn 16 and be eligible for my driver's license. Knowing my classmates, I was convinced that as soon as I slipped behind the Cadillac's steering wheel, I would immediately be greeted by ridicule and laughter, just as I knew that my not getting a license would cause a similar reaction. Either way, I did not believe I could bear it.

The following Saturday I went with my father to the art department, vowing not to leave there until I knew why I was being tormented. When I was younger, I had sometimes spent rainy Saturday's with him in the basement of the college's fine arts building where he had taught me to throw and glaze a pot, mix oil paints, and work a kiln.

It was also a place where we had been able to talk to each other in a way we never could anywhere else. As we worked, he would tell me stories, sometimes about Leonardo, who died lamenting the failure of his life, wishing that he had more time, or Michelangelo, who, after finishing one of the last statues he would ever create, had to be stopped by his apprentices from destroying it, because the statue "wouldn't breathe." The story he told most often, however, was about a potter in ancient China who invented a beautiful, dark-red glaze, only to find that pottery coated with the glaze would crack each time it was fired. The potter lowered and raised the temperature of the kiln, changed the composition of the pots, and even burned different kinds of wood. After years of failure, the potter threw himself into the kiln, where his final load of glazed pots was baking. Later, all of the pots his friends took out of the kiln possessed the dark-red color, and all were unbroken. The charred bones his friends found in the kiln had been the missing ingredient.

We had been throwing pots for about an hour when I felt the time was right.

"Why did you buy a Cadillac, Dad?" I asked. "Why not a Mercury or Plymouth, or even a Ford?"

My father walked over to the sink to wash his hands. I followed, not about to leave without an answer.

"You've got to tell me," I said.

He picked up a paper towel and dried his hands.

"Because owning a Cadillac shows exactly how far I've come from that mill village where I grew up."

"But, Dad," I said, not sure how what I was about to say would be taken. "It's got over a hundred thousand miles on it, hardly anything works the way it should, and it's the wrong color."

My father smiled.

"That's true. Maybe it also shows how far I have to go."

One month before I turned 16 my father, who had been carefully checking the used-car advertisements in the Asheville and Charlotte papers for months, traded cars again. This Cadillac was only seven years old, not ten like the other, and its interior and exterior were in much better shape than its predecessor. It did have its drawbacks, however. It was also gray, but a darker, gloomier gray, and only one of its electric windows would close all the way.

This car was the first I ever drove, and much of the humiliation I had expected became a reality. I found myself able to make my classmates laugh hysterically almost anytime they saw me behind the wheel of the big, dark-gray Cadillac, with three windows partially down even in the middle of winter. I drove only when I absolutely had to, and then I slumped behind the wheel in the feeble hope that I could hide myself. I watched with envy as my classmates drove their families' normal cars.

In the next two years my father traded cars three more times; all were Cadillacs. Each was newer and, despite some drawbacks, better. In the spring of my last year of high school, only two weeks before my senior prom, my father traded for the last of these.

I had just gotten home from track practice when he drove up, slowly turning into our driveway. As my father got out of the car, I noticed for the first time that his hair was almost completely gray. I had been so caught up in my own life that I hadn't even noticed. The car was a Cadillac Fleetwood, the "Cadillac of Cadillacs," according to the owner's manual I found in the glove compartment. It was a 1973, meaning the car was less than three years old, and the odometer had fewer than 30,000 miles on it, beating the previous family record by 20,000 miles. All the electric windows worked, and the interior looked almost new.

But, like all our Cadillacs, this one had its drawbacks too. The main one was its color—black. Why it was black became all too clear when I was putting the owner's guide back in the glove compartment and found a stack of business cards with "Harris Funeral Home, Charlotte, North Carolina" printed on them.

Well, time had proven Jimbo right. Nevertheless, I wasn't nearly as upset as I would have been two years earlier, for in my last half-year of high school I had gained a great deal of confidence in myself. The Cadillacs had been a godsend as far as my track career went. Instead of spending my afternoons and evenings cruising around Cliffside in a car, like so many of my classmates, I ran, sometimes more than a 100 miles a week in the winter of my senior year. Now, in the spring, after running several fast times in the mile, I was receiving letters from a dozen schools about possible track scholarships. Nothing was definite yet, but in my last race I had set a conference record while an assistant coach from Chapel Hill was in the stands.

I was just as hopeful about impressing another person in the stands that day—Laura Bryan—and after the meet I asked her to go with me to our senior prom. She accepted. But the confidence I had the day of the race quickly disappeared. I soon began to have second thoughts about my date. Did she realize that going to the prom with me meant going in my father's car? I agonized over this question and several times almost asked her.

I had never taken a girl out in one of our Cadillacs. The few dates I'd been on, I arranged it so I wouldn't have to drive. My date and I just met somewhere. But you couldn't just meet at your senior prom. I finally convinced myself that Laura knew what kind of car she would be riding in and didn't care. Perhaps, finally, I had overcome the stigma of my father's Cadillacs and was about to become a normal teenager. So even though I had just found out that our newest Cadillac didn't just look like a car used in a funeral but actually had been, I was not too worried. I was the best high school miler in western North Carolina, and one of the prettiest and smartest girls at Cliffside High was going to the prom with me. Not even a black, ex-funeral car could stop me now.

The weekend before my senior prom, my father decided to drive over to Shelby to see my grandmother. My mother, anticipating that he would spend most of the weekend at the art department, had already made other plans. Then he came into my room and asked if I wanted to go. I was surprised; he usually assumed that if I wanted to go I would be in the car when he backed out of the driveway. I told him yes, I always enjoyed going to see my grandmother, but that I would need to get back before too late to make some plans with Laura for the prom.

We visited until late afternoon. As we were driving away from my grandmother's house, we turned right, onto a street I had never been on before. It was an old section of town; dogwood and oak trees lined the sidewalks, and behind them were huge, two-story, wooden houses, five times the size of my grandmother's home a half-mile away. For a few seconds I thought my father had once again forgotten where he was going. But he slowed the Fleetwood down until it was barely moving and pointed out the window at the largest of the houses.

"That is where Old Man Calhoun lived, the owner of the mill, when I was growing up."

My father didn't say anything else. Instead, he stopped the car and stared up at the big, white house. We stayed there for about a minute, saying nothing. I looked at my watch. I was supposed to call Laura at 6:30. I broke the silence, telling my father that we needed to go.

The prom was the following weekend. We picked up our tuxedos at school on Friday, a tradition at our school, and on Saturday morning my mother drove to a greenhouse outside Cliffside and bought Laura's corsage. The sky had been overcast all day, and as I drove to Laura's house, it began to drizzle. Fortunately, my mother made me take an umbrella as I went out the door. I took having the umbrella with me as a good omen, ignoring the sky as a possible omen, too.

When I got to Laura's, her parents took our picture. I gave her the corsage, and she gave me a white carnation.

136

The umbrella kept Laura dry, and she said nothing about my family's newest car as we began the ten-mile drive to the country club. It was only seven o'clock, but because of the cloudy skies it was already getting hard to see. I looked over at Laura, and she smiled at me in a way that made my legs feel weaker than they had ever felt after a race. I turned on the Fleetwood's headlights. Everything was going too well to risk even the slightest chance of another driver not seeing me and wrecking what promised to be one of the most enjoyable nights of my life.

Though heavily traveled, the road to the country club was only two lanes. I hadn't felt the need to drive the Fleetwood before this evening, but I was soon wishing I had, for the steering wheel was much looser than the ones on our previous cars. This, along with the wet, narrow road, made me more and more nervous. The road was, except for a few curvy stretches, a 55-mile an hour zone, but I was only going 35. Soon a small line of cars was behind me, unable or unwilling to pass me on the rain-slick roads.

We were five miles from our destination when the first car coming from the other direction pulled off the road. I didn't think anything of it, figuring the driver was having car trouble. A quarter of mile further, however, two more cars did the same thing.

Around Cliffside, it had long been a custom when you met a funeral procession coming in the other direction to pull off the road as a sign of respect for the departed and the departed's family. Whether you knew the person or not did not matter. It was a matter of manners, which the people I grew up around took very seriously. Three more cars pulled off the road before I realized what was happening. At that moment I prayed to God that Laura Bryan wasn't as smart as I thought she was and would not realize why those cars were pulling off the road.

For a few more minutes she watched, puzzled, while several more cars did the same thing. Then she turned to me.

"They think this is a funeral, and that we're leading it! And you," she shrieked, pointing to my carnation, "they think you're the funeral director."

She started shaking with laughter. I was too upset to try to speak. I was suddenly back in the ninth grade. It didn't matter that I had set a conference record in the mile run and might get a scholarship to Chapel Hill. It wouldn't have mattered if I had set a world's record. And it certainly didn't matter that my prom date was Laura Bryan, for Laura, who was bent over with laughter at that very moment, would never take me seriously again.

Five minutes passed before I was able to ask her if she wanted to go back home. I was hoping she would say yes, but between spasms of laughter Laura told me she had to go now to tell everyone what had happened. I tore the carnation off my lapel and switched off the headlights, hoping to stop the pulloffs, each of which now caused Laura to howl even louder. I no longer cared if I had an accident or not. I was almost hoping for one. Death or serious injury seemed preferable to what awaited me at the prom.

Once we got there, Laura wasted no time telling the

story to everyone she could. After an hour of being the butt of the same joke, I hated her enough not to feel obligated to stay any longer. I told her I was leaving, and if she wanted to stay she would have to find her own way home. I had to stand near the punch bowl until she was sure she had a ride arranged. She came back a few minutes later with Jimbo Miller, now wearing the white carnation I had torn off. He had come alone and was only too happy to take Laura home.

I was back home before 9:30. I took the keys to what was now known as the "funeral director's car" and handed them to my father. When my mother asked why I was home so early, I didn't even answer her. I went to my room and locked the door.

The following Monday afternoon I went to the bank and withdrew all the money from my savings account. I had been saving it for college, but college was no longer the number-one priority in my life; never having to drive one of my father's Cadillacs again was. As soon as I left the bank, I went over to the Gulf station where a 1967 Volkswagen Beetle was for sale. I had the right amount of money, but Johnny Heddon, the owner of the station who also owned the Beetle, refused to sell it to me without my parents' permission. At first, my parents were reluctant, but I was so adamant—and, after all, it was my money— that they soon gave in. Two weeks later Chapel Hill wrote and offered me a full scholarship. I accepted and left Cliffside in mid-August, in my Volkswagen.

The Fleetwood was the last car my father ever bought. He died during my senior year at Chapel Hill. In the fall of

1981, the Fleetwood was broadsided when a college student ran Cliffside's one stop light. My mother, who was driving the car, was uninjured, but the Fleetwood was too damaged to justify repairing it. My mother bought a 1976 Ford Pinto with the insurance money.

I drove the Volkswagen for a decade, until it blew a rod and ended up in a junkyard outside Greenville, South Carolina. For weeks I prowled used car lots looking for a replacement, always gravitating to the battered gas-guzzlers on the back rows.

I settled on a 1978 Cadillac Coup De Ville. Two of the electric windows worked when I bought it four years ago. Now only one does, the left rear window.

This is the car I drove last spring when I came up from South Carolina to visit my relations. I spent the night at my mother's house in Cliffside, and the next day she and I drove over to Shelby, picked up my grandmother, and spent the day visiting kin. We ended up at the cemetery outside Cliffside. My grandmother placed some jonquils on my father's grave, flowers she picked that morning.

It was starting to get dark as we drove back into Shelby from the cemetery. My grandmother asked to ride down Lee Street to look at the dogwoods, which were now in full bloom. I didn't know where Lee Street was, but she gave me directions and five minutes later I was on the same street I had been on years earlier with my father.

"That's where the owner of the mill lived, wasn't it?" I asked my grandmother as I pointed to the biggest house. My grandmother nodded that it was. I suddenly realized I had stopped the car in the middle of the street. A car was coming up behind me, so I pressed the accelerator and drove down to the end of the block.

My grandmother looked out the window at the dogwoods. "You know," she said, "there is something about a dogwood in the spring that fills a body with hope. It makes you feel like all your dreams can still come true."

When she said that I thought of my grandfather, working most of his life in the card room of the cotton mill, breathing the cotton dust that eventually killed him, dreaming of a son who would never have to see the inside of a cotton mill, but never living long enough to see his dream come true, to see his son, my father teaching at a college.

I thought of my father sitting in the art class with the mill owner's daughter and the other children whose fathers were doctors or lawyers or store owners and whose mothers stayed home, who did not have to work in a cotton mill to make ends meet. My father, too, dreaming of a life beyond the mill village.

As I waited to turn left, the dogwoods held my gaze, their blossoms blazing, bright as dreams against the darkness.

Epilogue

The coffee pot is empty and the chickens are raising a ruckus. Randy says it's already an hour past their feeding time. Vincent and I get in the truck and head back to town. Some of the breakfast regulars are out on the sidewalk in front of Greene's Cafe. They all look like they still can't believe it's gone, like the fire was just a bad dream. I offer to take Vincent to his mom's, but he says he'll just get out in front of Greene's Cafe, or at least where it used to be. I need to talk to Cecil Hamrick about ordering some supplies, so I go ahead and park and walk across the road to the hardware store. When I come back out Vincent hasn't moved from where I let him out. He's just looking around, looking like he's lost something and if he just looks hard enough he can find it. But if he's lost something I don't have time to help him find it, at least not this morning. I've got a half-finished garage up near Casar that's going to stay that way until I put a hammer and nails to it. I crank up the truck and head up Highway Ten, watch Cliffside disappear in the rearview mirror.

About the Author

Ron Rash is the John Parris Chair in Appalachian Studies at Western Carolina University and the author of six novels, four other collections of short stories, and four collections of poetry. Rash is the winner of the Frank O'Connor International Short Story Award, the Sherwood Anderson Prize, the James Still Award of the Fellowship of Southern Writers, the Weatherford Award for Best Novel, the Fiction Book of the Year Award of the Southern Book Critics Circle. He is a two-time finalist for the PEN/Faulkner Prize and twice winner of the O. Henry Prize.